W9-BSF-153

Aria

Aria

Nassim Assefi

Harcourt, Inc.
Orlando Austin New York San Diego Toronto London

www.HarcourtBooks.com

Library of Congress Cataloging-in-Publication Data
Assefi, Nassim.
Aria/Nassim Assefi.—1st ed.
p. cm.
1. Iranian American women—Fiction. 2. Oncologists—Fiction.
3. Mothers and daughters—Fiction. 4. Children—Death—Fiction.
5. Bereavement—Fiction. 6. Voyages and travel—Fiction.
7. Consolation—Fiction. 8. Psychological fiction. I. Title.
PS3601.S74A75 2007
813'.6—dc22 2006025376
ISBN 978-0-15-101293-0

Text set in AGaramond
Designed by Cathy Riggs

Printed in the United States of America
First edition

K J I H G F E D C B A

For my friend, Pamela,

My aunt, Zoleykha,

My grandmother, Robab,

And for any other parent who has suffered the loss of a child.

Aria

Dust among stars, dear Mother, blind space
without words when words were the typed story
of my life, here's my last epistolary
news. Remember the two of us
at the black caldera, its precipice
and charred 'ohi'a trees in a slurry
of lava below, then the hard sea?
Of course you can't. It's your darkness
I drive through trying to find my way back.
Someplace on this road we saw orchids
growing from cinders the volcano
left behind: pale lavender like a flock
of imagined birds here where my car skids
and the pavement slips away and then *No.*

—JOAN SWIFT

CHAPTER I

4 Tir 1369
June 25, 1990

Yasaman Azizam,

Your letter broke our hearts. Baba does not sleep anymore. Truthfully, neither do I. He walks around the house at night like a sleepwalker searching for something he has lost. I tell him you are a grown woman. Thirty-five years old! You have your own life now, but in my heart this does not change anything. I say this only to make him feel better. You do not understand that no matter how old you are or how accomplished, you are still our only child, our baby *joon.* Nothing can change that. You are our love and our life even if we are far away. I do not know if you can really understand the strength of our love for you until someday, *insha'Allah,* you become a parent yourself. The love between parent and child is unequal. You can never love your parents more than they love you.

You may be American born, but, *azizam,* you are one hundred percent Irani in your blood and have been brought up in our culture. How can you disgrace yourself and your family by living with this Justin fellow before a proper marriage? How can you be so selfish and not think about your parents, who have sacrificed everything to bring you into this world? I want to tell you to not let him take away your precious jewels, that you should save yourself for your husband, but I think it is too late for that now. So I want to scream this now at my daughter, I want to shake you into listening to your mother, but what is the use? Your father, who cannot keep any secrets, even when he swears to keep them upon the grave of his mother, has not told a word of this to our family here. That is how ashamed we are.

Who is this character Justin, anyway? Who has tricked you into letting him move into your life? You tell me he is a high school teacher as if I should be proud. My dear lady doctor, you have the highest graduate degree possible. You went to the top schools. Do you not think that it is a step down to be with a man who does not have an MD or a Ph.D.? You need a man who is your equal, someone to challenge your brilliant mind. In my heart, I always hoped you would find a nice Iranian boy as good as yourself, but I did not let myself pray too hard for this. And I never dreamed you would be with a man from a broken family. Nobody recovers from the trauma of divorced parents. You say he is a wonderful man, kind, generous, and loving. I hope, *azizam,* that this is true. I hope he is worthy of you and makes you happy. But mostly I want to make sure he loves you enough to make the commitment of marriage. *Joony,* you should be thinking about having children at this age. Are you sure you are not wasting your time on a substandard man?

Americans have such a romantic and unrealistic picture of marriage in their heads. They think they must fall in love before marrying a man. Do you not see that they have it all wrong? Love comes with time, with really knowing each other, with suffering through your differences. Do you think I loved your father when I married him? No! It took me years before I knew what love is. And now we have been married almost fifty years. Just look at the divorce rates in America. More than half of married couples break off their commitment, even when they have children who will surely suffer. Americans do not stick by things. They want everything to be happy and easy all the time. They do not understand that marriage first means compromise.

Your father is an old man. This week, since your letter has arrived, I have seen him raise his fist in rage and protest this terrible situation as if he were a stubborn youngster again. "I do not care if she wins the Nobel Prize. Yasaman is a failure. She is dead to me if she never marries!" Maybe he is too harsh, your father. You have worked so hard all of your life, *joony,* but a part of what Baba says is true. No matter how great of a doctor you are, and I am sure that you are, you will always feel like a failure until you have a good husband and stable family life.

I blame myself for this. I should have taken you home to Iran after you finished medical school. I should have kept a closer eye on you and not let you become so Americanized. Like a fool, I even changed your name from Yasaman to Jasmine to make it easier for the *farangis* to say. I was younger then, very naive. I did not realize that simple changes like that could forever take our daughter away from us.

You must remember how much we gave up so that you could succeed. We left our friends, family, and country. Your father left his thriving business to make sandwiches in a deli and drive a taxi. He suffered the humiliation of being treated as a dirty, uneducated immigrant. I changed diapers and wiped the bottoms of retarded children left in institutions to pay our infertility doctors' bills. I, who had never had to work a day in my life, was raised in a house of servants, and taught English and French to private students just to keep myself busy.

Having a child was the only thing missing from our lives. We had the perfect life in Iran, except for you. We sold everything to come to the United States, so that we could have the best doctors. You cannot imagine the embarrassment we went through for this problem. Your father felt that he was not a real man or proper husband before making me pregnant. Everyone blamed me for not being able to carry out my wifely duties. Some backward relatives of your father's even suggested he get a second wife. We had to make our problem a public matter when we filed the papers for immigration. Afterward we went through so much testing, all the humiliating questions the doctors asked us. But we were very determined from the start. And after thirteen years of marriage, God finally brought you to us. But now I see our prize and joy destroyed because we left you in that immoral country alone.

Thank goodness your father cannot write English, and for once I am happy that you cannot read Farsi. As hard as these words sound to you from your own mother, know that your father would be one thousand times harsher. So listen to me, *dokhtaram.* Whatever you do, do not let yourself become pregnant with this Justin fellow unless you marry him. I beg you, do not mention his name again or remind us about your living situation. We are dying of embarrassment here and no one knows your dirty secret. Imagine if your uncles find out or if Mamani Joon, God rest her soul, had known about this before she died. Please do what I say. Know that we want the absolute best for you in this life.

Your maman loves you.

FEBRUARY 19, 1997

Aria Talahi Avery, 5, of Seattle died on February 17 in a motor vehicle accident. She was a kindergarten student at Lakeview Elementary. She is survived by her mother, Dr. Jasmine Talahi, Clinical Associate Professor of Oncology at the University of Washington. Memorial service to be held on South Beach, Discovery Park, on February 23 at 2 P.M. In lieu of flowers, donations accepted to Committee to Help Iranian Children & Orphans, c/o Nahid Kashef, PO Box 9347, Bellevue, WA 98004.

February 25, 1997

Dear Maman,

Might your resentment and detachment dissolve if you hear what tragedy has befallen your daughter? Or perhaps you will feel vindicated? My precious daughter, Aria, the love of my life, the product of my joyful union with Justin, has been killed. You have been robbed of a granddaughter.

Dear Mother,

My daughter, Aria, has died. Perhaps you will feel this is my due for living in the modern world, for rejecting my strict Muslim upbringing. You never reached that point of acceptance as a parent where you let your child fly with the wings and roots you provided. No, you never trusted me nor understood me. Instead, you used guilt to try to control me. But you have failed and here I am ALONE.

Maman,

When I was little, I used to sit beside Mrs. Kendall at the piano and feign sobs as she played that Chopin prelude in E minor. God knows I could have inherited your genes for the real thing, or perhaps I was just mimicking your bitter immigrant blues. But since then, I am with dry eyes. I seem to have adopted the stoic gaze of the Americans you despise, despite a monumental dose of bad luck. I had to have an abortion in college from a single accident. Then the love of my life and my future husband died suddenly in his sleep. And now, the worst possible fate: my daughter, Aria, has been killed.

My darling Aria is dead, Maman Joon, and so is my purpose in life.

Here is some news to add to your martyr complex, Mother. God has stolen from you the chance to meet your only grandchild.

Your accursed Yasaman

April 18, 1997

Dear Dottie,

I am in the desert to be far away. I need distance from the garden, the bulbs Aria planted never to see bloom, the spring she did not know.

I never told you this: the night before our uncharacteristically silent drive to the airport, I returned to that fatal corner. As the neighborhood slept, I retraced her steps. I crouched behind those rhododendron bushes for hours, now surrounded by daffodils. I imagined every possible angle of her run to home base. As the sun rose, sharp pains stabbed my chest when I did not see her faint bloodstains on the pavement, even though they had long since been washed away by the heavy rains. Somehow I expected to find some trace of her. The first time, I found her missing left shoe in the forget-me-nots by the Gregorys' basketball hoop. It was still warm with her touch. There was a tiny hole in the big toe. How had I not noticed this before? Am I a terrible mother? How had this happened?

I want nothing to do with Rainier Lane, the house. I cannot thank you enough for moving in to take care of things while I am away. I know you noticed that I did everything I could to avoid Aria's room, the entire upper floor. It is too much to see her things, never to be touched by her again. It is worse than you think, though. I actually changed my morning route to work to avoid passing by Lakeview Elementary. I skipped entire sections in the grocery store. At the hospital, I took convoluted paths through the underground parking lot so that I would not have to walk by University Daycare. All those children still alive.

When Emilia d'Oro put the keys to her Arizona cottage into my palm after grand rounds some weeks ago, she raved about this place. She claimed to find deep peace in the Sonoran Desert after her painful divorce and invited me to stay as long as I needed. Maybe that gave me a glimmer of hope. I was desperate to do something constructive. I needed a break from all the reminders of Aria's accident. I was never really drawn to the desert before, so who knows why I imagined it might be a healing space for me. I must admit there is something slightly appealing about it now: the scorching sun, the rough and inhospitable sand, and the cacti in their prickly solitude. The dry vegetation, empty spaces, and barren landscape echo my mood. Besides, travel has always been a solace for me, "my tranquilizer of choice," you called it once. So here I am. I hope you realize this is not a rejection of you. I love and appreciate you so much. I know that if there were any hope of getting on with my life in Seattle, you would have made me do it.

I came to the desert expecting dishwater grays and dust. Little did I know that there are so many flowers here: primroses, poppies, lupines, lilies, and many others that I cannot name. There are bees in the desert. Did you know this? They live in solitary tunnels.

Pliers are a must for any desert household as cactus spines make no hesitation about lodging themselves into human skin should they be ruffled. Cactus taxonomy would interest you most about this place: There are chollas named teddy bear (not for hugging), pencil (though the branches are more the size of a calligraphy pen), and devil (known to stop people in their tracks). Like the human body, cacti have spines and ovaries, areoles and tubercles. We are not separate.

Alas, there is no comfort for me here. It is like walking into a giant cathedral. I can admire the architecture, peer at the stained-glass windows, and even appreciate the fine paintings of Christ before his death by exsanguination. But I actually loathe the desert for its arid beauty.

To the Guatemalan highlands I go next. Ever since Justin first told me about his Peace Corps days, I have wanted to visit his village. More than this is my desire to feel close to Justin in a place that has had so much meaning for him. I need to tell him the story of our daughter.

Love,
Your Desert Bee

P.S. You can reach me by poste restante in Guatemala:

Jasmine Talahi
Lista de Correos
Quetzaltenango
Guatemala

April 21, 1997

Mamani Joonam,

Thirty-five years since I last inhaled your rosewater and cigarette scent, but I remember you vividly. I am an adult now, a doctor and mother even, but all I crave is to be an infant again swaddled by your love. Maman and Baba have not spoken to me in so long. They have given up on me. They feel betrayed that I stayed in America, that I never once came to see them in Iran. I must admit that Iran is the last place on earth where I belong. Now that you are not there, it feels pointless to go.

Oh, dearest grandmother, I have forgotten our secret language, but somehow I am sure you understand me anyway. How to tell you this terrible news? But I can talk to you with an open heart. The thought of you still comforts me. I confess that I have not had the nice, easy life in America that you envisioned for me. My beautiful girl, Aria, who inherited your wisdom and love for roses, is gone. Maman abandoned her before she was even born. Her poor American grandmother has been too ill to be involved in Aria's life. If you had been alive, I know you would have cherished her, saved her.

Once, while visiting our local nursery, Aria was mesmerized by the dark red petals of the pomegranate rose. She closed her eyes, smelled intensely, and insisted we plant that very bush in our garden. Of course I agreed. It was a sign that she had connected with you. She never tasted the tart, pithy fruit of my childhood, those glistening rubies you collected for me with your tireless, arthritic hands, but she knew.

There are so many things to wish for these days, Mamani Joonam. Where do I begin? First, that I had finished growing up by your side, or that we could have at least visited each other during our many years of separation. Those static-filled, painfully brief phone calls were too infrequent and inadequate to express my true feelings for you. Second, that I could have taken care of you when you were ill. Above all, I hope you know that I have loved you with all my heart since the day I was born. I shall never forget you.

Your Yasaman

May 1, 1997

My dearest Aria,

Mama has just landed in a country called Guatemala. It is in Central America, between North and South America, just below Mexico. Do you remember our trip to Oaxaca? The little sombrero I stuck on your head to protect you from the bright sun? You were just a baby, but maybe you can remember everything now. Mama has not forgotten your birthday. How could I? It is the best day of my life. I have been collecting birthday presents for you. So, come out, come out, wherever you are!

Love love love you,
Mama

May 4, 1997

My dear Justin,

Riding the buses in Guatemala is sensory overload. First there is the aggressive recruiting at the terminal. A little nod upon hearing your destination and before you know it, the conductor has whisked away your bag, tossing it like a hot potato to his assistant on the roof.

You must wonder what I am doing here, following your route to Ixcheltenango, mounting the stairs of what could have been my childhood school bus: a Blue Bird with a plaque above the driver's seat identifying it as property of the Alameda County Certified School District, 1966.

You must be thinking: Why now? Am I too late? Am I disturbed to be doing this? There are things I must tell you, and somehow it feels right to talk with you here where you spent two of the most formative years of your life. Where to start? How to recount the last six years for you? I might be going crazy, but I know this is the right thing to do.

There are three of us to a seat, sometimes four or five if the children sit on laps. Then there are those unlucky souls in the aisle whose knuckles are like clamshells from grasping the overhead bars. Not that they have any place to fall. We are packed like kernels on a corncob. There is no escaping human touch. Miraculously, the conductor makes his way to the back, collecting money, weaving through short, compact bodies like a fish in dense seaweed. Reaching the end, he exits through the emergency door and climbs to the roof while the bus moves forward at full speed. On his stomach, he slithers his way to the front of the bus and hoists himself back into the door when we stop. I feel like this conductor operating at dizzying speed, only I do not know where I am going.

At the crossroads, as soon as the bus slows, there is an invasion by troops of young girls and boys carrying loads of food and drink on their heads. *"Chuchitos, chuchitos. Aguas, aguas. Maní, maní."* The clever ones climb up the sides of the bus. They offer their goods through an open window. One- and two-quetzal notes fly between hands.

Do you remember our "Ode to Conception" party? How silly our invitation sounds now, but we were giddy with love. You always had a way of bringing out the lighthearted girl in me.

> *Outwitting the steadfast guardians of zygote formation, Justin's plucky sperm has conspired with Jasmine's maverick of an ovum. The rumors are true: We are pregnant! You are not the only ones who are stunned. Nature (i.e., faulty birth control) has disregarded our carefully constructed calendar and will deliver our baby sometime around Mother's Day.*
>
> *We will soon get our act together for a wedding of some sort, but in the meanwhile, Jasmine's retching—enough to last her a lifetime of empathy with her cancer patients—demands libations to the nausea goddess! We will provide food and drink in exchange for your favorite fertility poem.*

The yellow bus is decorated with bright red paint and big green letters on the side that read: "AMOR PROHIBIDO." If you only knew how our forbidden love permanently changed my relationship with my family, you might have convinced me to leave you. But then there would be no Aria. No Aria. No Aria. No.

Stuck to the windshield in shiny black, reflector letters is "DIOS ESTA CONMIGO." I wish I could feel God with me now. The truth is that I never understood your faith, not just in God, but in all things.

Almost every commercial vehicle in Guatemala makes some religious claim, even those with "ESTÚPIDO ROMÁNTICO" and "LOVE-MACHINE PLAYBOY" painted on the sides. Was this true twenty years ago? How preposterous that the "VIRGIN MARY" and "SEXY SENSUAL" are stickers on the same bus! Were I a bus, what shiny slogan would be plastered on my windshield for all to see? It would not be "DIOS ME GUÍA." Perhaps "VIRGEN DEL CAMINO," because nothing in this life has prepared me for this. I am a virgin to these roads.

On May 10, 1991, I gave birth to Aria Talahi Avery. At forty-one weeks, I was beginning to lose hope that I would ever deliver, especially when everyone was telling me that pregnant doctors often have preterm labor. The contractions began in the middle of the eleven o'clock news. At first they felt like intense stretches. I woke up Dottie, and she was like an expectant parent herself. She ran the bubble bath. I had packed my hospital bag weeks earlier. Dot put on the Chopin impromptus and paged the on-call masseuse with the kind of excitement I imagined only you could have.

Between contractions, Dot washed my hair and handed me the navy silk pajamas you had ordered for me for Christmas. They were beautiful and elegant, the perfect outfit for laboring. Thank you, my love, for your thoughtfulness to the very end. I still have those pj's. Dot groans every time she sews up another hole in them. The masseuse arrived after all this pre-labor primping. She rocked me back and forth, moving her hands in the direction of the contractions. She massaged my swollen feet, furrowed brow, and tense scalp. She coached me to breathe through the pain. Taxol and Bleo hid beneath the couch, afraid of my deep-throated cries. I was more animal than human.

By the time my water broke and I reached the hospital, I could not imagine going au natural and immediately ordered an epidural. Before the anesthesiologist's arrival, violent waves of pain overtook my body. In the midst of it, I wanted to strangle the masseuse because I could not stand to be touched. Dot tried to excuse her from the room, but it was too late. The poor woman witnessed my outbursts and was so startled that she left without taking her CD of the African Divas. Then retrograde amnesia (the only thing I remember now are those tribal birthing songs), because the next thing I knew, tiny, perfect Aria was lying on my chest, seven pounds, eleven ounces, and twenty inches, Apgar scores to make you proud.

Your absence has been palpable at every moment but especially in those early days. Of course Mamani Joon could not be with me either. Maman and Baba chose not to greet their beautiful granddaughter upon her arrival. Nevertheless, there were moments when I felt like the happiest woman alive: I finally had a relative in this country again.

Love,
Jasmine

May 10, 1997

Aria Aria Aria Aria Aria Aria Aria Aria
Aria Aria Aria Aria Aria Aria Aria Aria
Aria Aria Aria Aria Aria Aria Aria Aria
Aria Aria Aria Aria Aria Aria Aria Aria
Aria Aria Aria Aria Aria Aria Aria Aria
Aria Aria Aria Aria Aria Aria Aria Aria
Aria Aria Aria Aria Aria Aria Aria Aria
Aria Aria Aria Aria Aria Aria Aria Aria
Aria Aria Aria Aria Aria Aria Aria Aria
Aria Aria Aria Aria Aria Aria Aria Aria
Aria Aria Aria Aria Aria Aria Aria Aria
Aria Aria Aria Aria Aria Aria Aria Aria
Aria Aria Aria Aria Aria Aria Aria Aria
Aria Aria Aria Aria Aria Aria Aria Aria
Aria Aria Aria Aria Aria Aria Aria Aria
Aria Aria Aria Aria Aria Aria Aria Aria
Aria Aria Aria Aria Aria Aria Aria Aria
Aria Aria Aria Aria Aria Aria Aria Aria
Aria Aria Aria Aria Aria Aria Aria Aria
Aria Aria Aria Aria Aria Aria Aria Aria
Aria Aria Aria Aria Aria Aria Aria Aria
Aria Aria Aria Aria Aria Aria Aria Aria
Aria Aria Aria Aria Aria Aria Aria Aria
Aria Aria Aria Aria Aria Aria Aria Aria
Aria Aria Aria Aria Aria Aria Aria Aria
Aria Aria Aria Aria Aria Aria Aria Aria

Happy sixth birthday, my sweetest of sweetie pies.
Mama misses you and loves you so much.
I promise to find you very, very soon.
P.S. Please give me a hint about where you are.

May 13, 1997

Dear Alexander,

In Guatemala I have been inducted into your family's cult of corn. The Mayan world revolves around maize with a capital *M.* According to legend, humankind was created from maize. It is the dietary staple but possesses as much spiritual nourishment as physical. It has been a full immersion experience. I breakfast with *tamalitos* (maize dough cooked in maize leaves) and *atol* (maize gruel with generous amounts of sugar and cinnamon). I lunch with tortillas (maize pancakes), wrapped in napkins as warm and snug as a child on a mother's back. I snack with *chuchitos* (tamales stuffed with vegetables and chili pepper) and roasted corn (with lime and salt), and then dine with more tortillas. It is no surprise that Guatemalan novelist Miguel Ángel Asturias won the Nobel Prize for, among other works, *Hombres de maíz* (*Men of Maize*). I, too, am made of maize now.

At the fiesta we obtained the earth's permission before the seeds were sown; I lit candles for you, desperately hoping for your well-being. The villagers burned candles honoring water, animals, and the universe. The planting itself was a community affair. Men, women, and children worked together. Even the elderly participated. Those who were too old for the manual labor served *atol* and tamales, and others told stories to keep spirits high. I carried you with me during the night watch as I chased away the rodents and raccoons hungry to dig up the seeds. Your hands were with me each morning, a final parting, as I raked the soil with my fingers, sensing the temperature of the earth, learning to make predictions about the sprouting of the first leaves.

Working the earth in Guatemala, I have imagined you countless times as a child on your farm in Platte, your father coaxing you away from a book to join in the water-setting contests in the days before piped irrigation. You would halfheartedly participate among the mob of family, while your brother would win every season. Your parents would be impressed with my new vocabulary: *tuza, xilote, mazorca, milpa.* Especially since this city girl only just learned her corn anatomy in English last Christmas. They would be thrilled by the sacredness of each tassel, shank, silk, stalk, and ear. I would make them proud, the way I brag about Nebraska being one of the largest producers of maize in the United States.

Why do I perseverate on these details when all I want to do is apologize? Oh, Alex, I regret so many things: how I handled that last night with you, terminated communication without explanation, and made you believe that it was possible to continue life as we had known it. Our last night together, I fought like hell to convince myself that the old Jasmine could return, that it was possible to move beyond all that had happened. The next morning I knew it was an illusion.

Please try to proceed with your life. It is better that we cease communication. Know that I have loved you deeply and will forever cherish the memories of our time together.

It is not surprising that after the worst possible turn of events in my life, I find myself working in the cornfields, as you did in your childhood. I hope you can see this as I do, a celebration of our relationship, a communion on a deep, earthbound level, carrying you within me even as I say good-bye.

Love,
Jasmine

May 17, 1997

Dear Justin,

After what feels like days of riding the bus, Guatemala has become as familiar to me as the human body. There are cities divided into gridlike streets, suffocating from automobile exhaust and burning coal. Banks and chain-food restaurants, like McDonald's, Taco Bell, and Wimpy's, are flanked by steel-faced security guards, arms resting lightly on their machine guns, a remnant of the violence. You would be so happy to know that peace accords were finally signed last year. I remember your stories about the men from Ixcheltenango who simply disappeared, the grieving families they left behind. Only now I get it.

The majority of Mayan Indians continue to live in the highlands. You described their weekly market as a bouquet of colors, and how right you were. I found everything from hand-embroidered costumes to pirated baseball caps that said L.A. Gear, live chickens to yellow mango slices on a stick sprinkled with red chili pepper. The volcanic cone in the backdrop of the plaza looks almost surreal. So do the steep terraced farms: "the green waterfalls," you called them. Your fondness for marimba brings me to the market in search of the warm xylophone sounds and makes me feel like you are listening to what I have to say. Am I delusional? Am I still your kitten? What happens to love when one person goes away?

On one of the buses, a young mother with her three-year-old daughter sat beside me. The little girl had pigtails and small gold hoops in her ears. Mucus dribbled down her nose and her head crawled with lice. Nevertheless, I could not keep myself from touching her. I coaxed the little girl to sit on my lap. When her mother looked away, I kissed her rosy cheeks three or four times. While she stared with distrust at the German tourists sitting in back of us, she seemed to think of me as one of the family. What I really wanted to do was hold her tightly, to be reminded of what it feels like to have a little girl against my breast.

When Aria was three, she had already declared her curious and bold personality in stark contrast to the docile daughter that I was. There was no end to Aria's questions, and she could engage you, even against your will, until she got an answer that satisfied her. On a flight to San Juan Island this past Thanksgiving, she asked me this in quick succession: "Mama, how do planes fly? Why do the wings not flap? Who drives the plane? How come there are no birdies up here?" I was exhausted after a night of being on call with a young patient who had nearly bled to death from his leukemia. I must have mumbled something in my sleep that was not entirely satisfactory to this tenacious daughter of ours. I awoke with a start to find Aria missing from her seat. She had made her way to the cockpit and politely began asking her questions of the pilot. Not only did he humor her, but he also guided her hands on the control panels.

I miss her most as a physical being: her silky forehead, her protuberant belly button, the way her eyes would turn to crescent moons when she looked at something that deeply interested her, her limp weight in my arms, how she molded herself to my body in those infant days. For so long our communication was not transmitted through words, but you would not believe it if you saw her affinity for reading. At bedtime it was always: "One more book, Mama, one more book." She inherited my father's skill for bargaining. "One more book" meant at least two more, and then finally I would kiss that soft, angelic brow, marveling at its innocence and receptivity to the world, and she would accept her assignment to sleep. "Good night, Aria. I love you." "I love you most, Mama."

I do not want you to think that motherhood was always easy for me. There were numerous times when I felt like a failure. For example: One morning Aria opened up her panda backpack, looked into her lunch bag, and threw it onto the table. "No more turkey," she said, "I want lunch like Akiko." I was in a foul mood already, running late, with no understanding of what she meant. I ordered her to stop being so unreasonable. She began to cry without pause. Where was this coming from? Did she not feel loved enough? Maybe this was about missing you?

Suddenly, I felt guilty. I envisioned University Daycare writing a note in their monthly report card: "Your daughter could benefit from more creative lunches. She seems short-changed by her daily routine of turkey sandwich, carrot sticks, and fruit when her classmates enjoy far more interesting and varied cuisine." I felt so inadequate that I caved in to her demands. I stopped at the Co-op and let her pick out a lentil burrito and giant oatmeal raisin cookie.

In the middle of an exhausting day at work that had started badly, I called Aria's teacher and begged for the details. I simply had to know: What was so special about Akiko's lunches? She told me about the red lacquered bento box, its distinct compartments for sushi rolls, seaweed salad, pickled ginger, wasabi, edamame beans, and orange slices. It turns out that Akiko's grandmother fusses over her lunches each day. Apparently, there is even a tiny origami animal with every lunch. How could Aria not be jealous?

When I was Aria's age, my Mamani Joon, like Akiko's grandmother, made me feel like the most important person alive. She was my guardian angel. Hers was the bed to which I ran after a bad dream or stomachache. My poor little Aria had only one mother with no time to spoil her. If you were here, I know you would have balanced my shortcomings, diluted the miserable moments. Truthfully, though, I needed you more to witness the joy: seeing Aria plant a bulb in the garden, attempting her first *A* as a lefty, or feeling her plump thighs wrapped around your waist . . . I missed you most then.

You once remarked that Guatemala is a country of extreme contrasts. I see it now. There are lowlands beside highlands, lush rain forests and scrubby beaches not far apart from each other. A freezing morning ends in a sultry afternoon. Mayan ruins are in close proximity to colonial Spanish architecture. Traditional costumes hang beside

T-shirts with misspelled English-language logos. Pedro de Alvarado (leader of the Spanish conquistadores) and Tecún Umán (chief of the Quiché warriors) are names of bars on the same street. With every café, gas station, and discotheque branded by the Orange Crush insignia, not to mention Guatemalan teeth in utter disrepair, you might think the soda company owns the country. However, the low city buildings with gaping cracks in their facades and the paucity of skyscrapers remind you that it is really the earthquakes that rule this place. The awesome power of nature is undiminished by faith or good acts or admirable intent. It is not affected by the sudden absence of our daughter or the decimation of entire villages. Or do you still believe in a loving God who has a hand in all things? Whose prognoses for humankind are translated as fate?

As an oncologist, I, too, have been humbled by nature. I tried to shield our daughter from my work, but occasionally she sensed what was going on. A few months ago one of my favorite patients, a feisty Ibo-speaking woman from Nigeria, succumbed to her ovarian cancer, despite surgery and several rounds of aggressive chemotherapy. She and I never spoke directly without the use of an interpreter, but we had a deep connection that made words seem almost unnecessary. When I came home that day, Aria was especially attentive. She hopped onto my lap, twisted a strand of my hair around her finger, let it go with a *boing,* and insisted that she had a secret to tell me, as long as I promised not to repeat it. "No telling a soul, Mama. Cross your heart, hope to die, stick a needle in your eye." After my solemn oath of secrecy, Aria started to whisper as if she were about to tell me something vitally important, so that I actually worried about what she might say. Then she kissed my ear with such loud, slurpy noises that I could not help but to burst into laughter. Suddenly, she got quiet and ran her fingers down my face, her own eyes round and expressive as if she were feeling my tears: "Mama, I love you most."

There was a kind of wisdom in this five-year-old child of ours that continues to amaze me. As if she came from another world.

Love,
Jasmine

May 20, 1997

Dearest Aria,

Since you have been gone, I have been remembering important stories about our family that I want to share with you. Your great-grandmother, my Mamani Joon, came to America for the first time when her eldest son, your grandfather, was going to become a father. Mamani Joon always blamed my maman for not having a baby sooner. Maman soon forgave her mother-in-law when she saw how my grandmother doted on me. Mamani Joon lived with us until I was seven, and she was the one who took care of me. Mamani Joon never went to school, but she was so smart. She tricked me into speaking her Persian language. She would not let me watch TV because that would pollute my native tongue. She pretended that she did not speak English so that I was forced to respond to her in Persian. My first word was with her: *"Gol, gol, gol."* I said it as if I had made a big discovery, pointing to the flowers in our garden. Mamani Joon had a magical thumb in the garden, just like you.

Mamani Joon loved garage sales. This embarrassed Maman, who was ashamed of buying other people's used stuff. All week Mamani Joon's eyes were on the lookout for those bright signs: GARAGE SALE, MOVING SALE, and ESTATE SALE. Though she had trouble reading the English alphabet, she could make out those words from a mile away. Mamani Joon would follow Maman around our apartment during the weekend and did not leave her alone until she had been to at least three or four sales. Mamani Joon never kept what she bought for herself. No, she was collecting gifts for our family in Iran.

Mamani Joon had a secret way of knowing things. The night before I was born, two weeks before I was due to arrive, friends of the family asked Mamani Joon if she wanted to accompany them for a weekend at the casinos in Las Vegas. Your great-grandmother loved gambling even more than she did garage sales. She was usually the one to request a trip to Vegas but not that night. "My granddaughter is making her entrance into this world tomorrow," she said. "I want to be there to welcome her."

"But, Ameh Joon," said the Iranian friend, addressing my grandmother as a dear aunt, "the doctors have told us that your grandchild will not be born for another two weeks." Nevertheless, Mamani Joon stayed home, packing Maman's overnight bag for her and greeting me the following day with a devoted smile that would imprint itself on my soul.

Once I grew up and started going to school, your great-grandmother grew lonely. I was away from home most of the day and she had no one to talk to. Maman tried to convince her to visit with other old ladies in the community center, but Mamani Joon got so mad that she spit on Maman's face. That was it. All of their past arguments had not been enough to make my baba ask his mother to leave. But it was clear now. Mamani Joon had disrespected his wife. She must return to Iran.

When I found out that Mamani Joon was leaving, I cried for days. Mamani Joon was my playmate, my cheerleader, and my best friend. Oh, how she used to tell me stories about the home country. I told her that one day I would visit her in Iran, but it never happened. Now I have run out of tears. I keep waiting for the two of you to return. Hurry back, sweet pea.

Love,
Your mama

May 28, 1997

Dear Justin,

Indigenous life in Guatemala is rooted in the earth, you once told me. Now I understand this. I have spent the past month in Ixcheltenango helping the community with their planting of maize. When I mention your name, their faces light up and their tongues rapidly click in the guttural sounds of Mam. We are unable to communicate well enough for me to tell them about what happened to you. It is for the best. Rarely I hear a word in Spanish that I understand like *agua,* and then I know they are probably referring to your work with water sanitation. We barely speak, these Mayans and I, but then again, working the soil is one of the most universal ways of communicating. We treat the earth the best way we know how, plant the seeds lovingly after a ceremony asking permission to do so, and then wait with an inherent trust in the soil to do its job. The soil complies for the most part, assuming no freak occurrences in weather patterns or natural disasters.

At the one-week mark, I gently raked my hands through the ground, not believing the growth of the seeds beneath my fingers. According to my environmentally conscious guidebook, farmers whose livelihood depends on maize have overused the soil here, and its fertility is nearly depleted. On the twelfth morning after the planting, the matriarch of the family, a grandmother named Concepción who remembers you well, was with me when the sprouts made their first appearance. With a toothless smile and a magenta ribbon woven through her hair, she grabbed my shoulder, her hand moving down my arm as she pulled me to the new greenness. I touched it with some hesitation, as if still skeptical of its existence. Two callused palms, caked with dirt, covered my hand as if to say, "You see, dear, the earth always comes through for us."

Dottie came through for us in the most remarkable way. She convinced me to move to Seattle so that I would not have to raise our daughter alone. She became a kind of second parent to Aria. I remember making Dr. Noori do another ultrasound two weeks after your death to prove to myself that our baby was still alive. It was so hard going through with it, remembering you there for the first one, holding my hand and grinning widely. I thought this much grief would surely be cardiotoxic to the baby and me, but through some miracle of human resiliency, we kept on keeping on.

The day Aria finally came to terms with your absence was at the Westlake Center while we were Christmas shopping. She was so adamant about wanting to sit in Santa's lap that I agreed to the half-hour wait in a line full of hyperactive children, though you know I do not usually have the patience for that sort of thing. She told Santa what she wanted in such a low whisper that I could not hear a word of what she said. While the elves helped her climb aboard the metal Rudolph, Santa motioned for me to come closer. "Come here, Aria's mom. I have a special Christmas message for you." I thought to myself, What is going on here? Is this standard Santa protocol? "Little Aria said that the only thing she wants for Christmas is a daddy. I thought you should know." Needless to say, there was no "ho, ho, ho" or "Merry Christmas" following our conversation.

I thanked him and caught our child as she jumped from Rudolph's saddle. There was no evidence of the longing Santa had described. In fact, she was bouncing around with excitement. "Mama, Mama! I made his nose light up. Bright red! Did you see it?" We went home and I fixed her some hot cocoa. She has your sweet tooth. Then I called up Dottie, who came over right away to watch Aria while I went to the library.

I leafed through book after book, searching for the right way to explain your death to her. There were titles like *When God Calls Us to His Pastures* and *Benny Sitting Shiva,* and books that portrayed death like a long, long nap, not unlike Sleeping Beauty's spell. In my head I replayed the words of Aria's pediatrician. "We live in a culture that denies death. We have memorial services instead of funerals. We say 'passing away' instead of 'dying.' Less than fifty years ago, death used to be considered an inevitable and natural part of life. Now it is as often ascribed to personal negligence or bad luck." She told me that parents often feel more comfortable discussing sex and childbirth with their children than having a frank discussion about death. That they use euphemistic language from long ago when it was chic to have your kids believe in Santa Claus or the boogeyman. She made it clear to me that children are confused by these falsehoods. She urged me to tell Aria about your death. "Tell her simply and gently, but also honestly."

Aria and I had already discussed this subject many times before. One day Aria asked me out of the blue if her day-care teacher was Daddy. When I shook my head, she said, "Okay then, Mama, is it Mr. Saito?" She had just started her Suzuki violin classes then, and Mr. Saito, her teacher, had a fatherly feel to him. I was actually surprised she did not suspect Daddy was my boyfriend Alexander. I met him three years ago at the book signing of Nawal El Saadawi, the Egyptian doctor and political activist. Alex had actually interviewed her about founding the Arab Women's Solidarity Association while she was imprisoned in the early eighties. Though he looks obviously gringo, he has this gentle way of approaching strangers that makes them feel instantly comfortable around him, no matter what part of the world he is in or how intimidating his camera and notepad. The funny thing is that he is not nearly as at ease around children, and Aria sensed that.

I told Aria all about you again. I started from the very beginning. Showed her all of the pictures. I moved the large framed photo of the two of us, the one from our last trip to Ansel Adams Wilderness, from the living room and hung it above her bed. I told her you loved her very much but had died when she was still growing in my uterus. She looked so sad for a moment that I was sure she understood. Then she said, "Mama, when is Justin Daddy coming back?"

So I tried explaining in different ways. We talked about

flowers that dried up and died. We discussed the death of her goldfish, Oscar. Until she finally understood that death meant never returning. Then came weeks of questions about you. "Mama, what was Daddy wearing when he died? Did it hurt him to die? Where do dead people live?" Finally, the questions subsided, although once in a blue moon she would say things like "Did Daddy like Oreo cookies too? Would you let him eat them?"

At the library I finally found the right book. *Saying Goodbye* is a story of a girl whose father dies in the hospital. It is realistic but not too stark. It starts with the joy of the child's birthday, a celebration of the beginning of life, and then begins talking about the end of life. There are hospital scenes and pictures of the girl and mother being sad. In the end, it affirms life over death, assuring the girl that most people will live to a very old age. It was exactly what Aria needed.

I returned home to find Aria and Dottie setting up a fort between the living-room couches. I gathered them by the fireplace in the library, and together we read the book. This sharp cookie of ours was already such a good reader. When we reached the end of the book, the tears came. Aria cried like an adult who had finally let go. Belly sobs that turned Dot and me into waterfalls.

"Mama, are you going to die?" She looked at me in a panic. "Aunt Dottie, are you going to die?" I pulled her onto my lap and wrapped my arms around her. Dot stroked her hair. I reassured her: "Not until we are old, old ladies with white hair and glasses hanging around our necks, and you have children of your own." My voice was creaky, like when I read the grandmother part in "Little Red Riding Hood." She seemed okay with that. Her teachers told me that at playtime many of her dolls died and she wanted to bury them outside. That eventually stopped. I never imagined it would be Dot and me who would need the comforting.

Just before Aria's accident, we went to visit your tree in Discovery Park, the grand madrone where I sprinkled some of your ashes. Somehow, this majestic tree facing the sailboats passing along the Puget Sound captures your spirit. Aria brought her watering can, though I assured her there is more than enough rain during a Seattle winter to water your tree. It was one of those unusually sunny days in February, where you could see both Mount Rainier and the Olympic Mountains. Aria gave her palm a kiss and blew it into the horizon. Then she hugged the tree trunk as tight as she could, scrunching up her face as if she were making great effort. "What was that for?" I asked with curiosity. The week before she had started to say that her kisses were flavored. So I would humor her. I would smack my lips, chew an imaginary kiss for a few seconds, and then name the taste. "It was a chocolate kiss for Daddy."

Dot has always questioned whether our "contraceptive failure" child was really unplanned in the grand scheme of things. She thinks Aria is indelible evidence of our love for one another. I sometimes get impatient with her romantic notions of how the world works, but I must admit wanting to believe her on this one.

Justin, how I wish you had been here to see our child. You would have delighted in her so. We both miss you very, very much. But wherever you are, you are woven into our lives. Like that madrone, our roots are tangled in your soil.

Love,
Jasmine (and Aria)

June 5, 1997

Dearest Aria,

When I was seven years old, my Mamani Joon returned to Iran. On our last day together, she took me out for a walk around Stow Lake in the Golden Gate Park, and there we sat on a bench watching the birds. From her handbag, she pulled out two ruddy pomegranates. She showed me how to squeeze the seeds in the fruit without bursting the skin. As we gently softened our pomegranates, my grandmother told me: "This pomegranate is like you, my love. It, too, is a child of Iran. Only it is at least four thousand years old." I looked at my grandmother with wide-eyed amazement as I tried to think about being four thousand years old and then continued to dig my two thumbs into the round fruit.

"When those Christians tell you that Eve picked an apple from the Garden of Eden, do not believe them. The pomegranate was the only fruit in that garden." I was not quite sure what she was referring to, but I listened carefully anyway. "Even our Prophet Muhammad advised us to eat the pomegranate because he believed that the tart fruit would cleanse our spirit." She told me about the cherry-colored pomegranate flowers, how they guard their fruit from insect attacks like the fiercest of mothers. "When I have disappeared from this earth, I want you to think of me every time you bite into the pomegranate and suck out its juices."

My grandmother looked away and went back to inspecting her fruit. There was not a single mark on its rough texture. Meanwhile, I was far behind in my preparation to suck out the pomegranate juice and began pounding the fruit on the bench like a hammer. "Be careful, my soul," she said. "The blood of pomegranates can stain you permanently. You must honor history. For thousands of years, before the invention of doctors, we have used every part of the pomegranate to heal ourselves." Mamani Joon handed me her pomegranate and started working on mine. "You cannot be rough with this fruit. Be patient. Work with it gently. As you suck the refreshing juice, let the sweetness remind you of all that is good in your life. With the sweetness, you will also taste the sour seeds. That is normal. That is to be expected. Suffering is a part of life, my child. We can taste the depths of sweetness only after we have swallowed the sour." Then she kissed me and hugged me, taking away all of my sadness. At the time I was not quite sure what she meant by these words nor why she had shared them with me, but I decided to remember them anyway. Now I pass them on to you, my love, with hopes that the wisdom of my grandmother will protect you, wherever you are.

Love,
Mama

June 10, 1997

Dear Justin,

It has taken me countless letters to work my way up to what happened to Aria, but I am finally ready. On February 17, at approximately 4:10 P.M., a teenage driver swerved around the corner and hit Aria. Our daughter was playing kick the can with the neighborhood children. She did not survive.

How I wish that I could believe in paradise, some divine plan for eternity. It would be so comforting to know that she was with you. You would recognize her in an instant. She has your same lopsided smile, your cheeky almond eyes, your love for the natural world, and your goofy sense of humor.

I was already at the hospital. They paged me out of a patient room: Danny Yang, lung cancer. The emergency room visit was brief. There were papers to sign. I returned home. I photographed the tire marks from every direction. I hunted for clues. I saw the blood. I documented the damage to the Gregorys' garden. I tried to interview the children who had witnessed the accident. At the McGoverns', Eleanor opened the door and hugged me for what felt like hours. She said the girls were too upset to talk about it. Maybe later. I vowed to interrogate each and every child who was there in the coming days. I called Dot.

Days passed. I am not sure what happened. Aria is dead?

Dot was the one who made me walk into her room. I managed to avoid it for three days, as if she had only gone away for a weekend with Akiko's family. Dot literally pushed me up each step. On the door hung Aria's handprint in clay, a project she had done for Mother's Day at day care last year. I walked silently through the room. I inspected like a detective. Dot waited outside. I leafed through her books. I picked up a purple crayon from the floor and put it back into its case. I touched her bright orange bird, Dodo, with stuffing coming out at one side. I opened her closet and organized her little shoes the way I always do. Her pink Keds, the last ones she wore, were still safely under my pillow.

When I reached her perfectly made bed, I sank to my knees. I put my head on her pillow. I could actually smell her, Justin. There it was: the fresh, sweet scent that a mother knows so well. I had pointed to my cheeks and demanded my usual postbath kisses before I put her to bed the night that would be her last. I had a vivid image of her succumbing to sleep. She always slept on her side, in a kind of fetal position. She was the most beautiful child. I used to check on her during the night. I marveled at the soft curve in her spine, that such sweet passivity could coexist with boundless energy.

I touched the bed and she was not there. I started to sob: "Oh god, oh god. Come back, Aria. Please, baby, come back."

Dot came in then. She squeezed my shoulders and commanded me with all the authority of a general: "Let it out." I did. I was always good at following directions. I do not know how long we stayed there, but by the time we left, there was a small puddle on her bedspread. I surrendered to exhaustion. I did not think it was physiologically possible for a person to cry that much.

Every time I am forced to envision the future without her in it, I get light-headed. Sharp pains pierce through my body. I keep trying to convince myself that this is all psychosomatic. For Christ's sake, I am a doctor. I have witnessed this phenomenon countless times in my patients' lives. How to explain that knowing the mechanism, believing that this is all illogical and being able to chart the map of grief's stages, does not help me at all.

After the accident the barista at Espresso Express looked at me with such melancholy eyes that I had no choice but to drop my macchiato and watch with glee as it stained the pristine hospital lobby floor. An elderly Ethiopian woman custodian saw what happened and approached me to clean up the mess. She patted me on the shoulder as if to say, "No worry, sweetheart, these things happen." I hissed back with all the venom I could mobilize: "I do not want your pity!" Every patient in the ENT waiting room turned to stare at me, and I felt some satisfaction at the scene I had caused. My eternally optimistic hairdresser was the next subject of my wrath. He called me after reading Aria's obituary and tried to comfort me: "Honey, you are still young. There is so much of life for you to live. Time will heal this tragedy. You know, you can always adopt a child." I did not respond for a minute so that he actually queried whether I was still on the line. Finally, I responded: "Aria was my future," and hung up the phone.

I am dissociating, as shrinks say. My cerebral cortex knows that she is gone for good, and yet I keep seeing her in odd places. As I eat *tamalitos,* she runs through the door, jumps into my lap, and throws her arms around me, saying, "Mama, Mama, guess what? I'm back! Did you miss me? Give me a bite!" Or working in the fields, I hear her singing "America the Beautiful."

My concentration was once so sharp I could dictate every detail of a patient's history, even after seeing twenty of them in a day. Now I have to resort to leaving notes around the house to remember the most banal tasks: brush teeth, take vitamins, empty garbage. Dot could not believe the extent of my absentmindedness until she watched me try to heat a microwave dinner without removing it from the box. Two days later I folded all of my dirty laundry and put it away.

The real Jasmine is gone. She and Aria are back in Hawaii. Aria has smeared herself with violet and turquoise body paint and insists on painting my body too. She has appointed herself queen and made me her little princess. Upon Aria's suggestion, we make sand castles for all the girls and women in Iran, so they can romp around freely without their veils. It is a different world now. Can you believe she never experienced sexism? In her world the figures of authority were female: her teacher, principal, pediatrician, and even the senator who came to Lakeview Elementary for a special assembly.

Even basic chores, like grocery shopping, became unbearable after February 17. Roberta, the clerk at Whole Foods, thought she was making small talk while waiting for me to write a check and asked: "Where is that spunky kiddo of yours?" I fumbled with my pen and almost vomited on the cash register.

I fantasized saying: "Aria is doing great. Right now she is playing at a friend's house. She is graduating from kindergarten this June. Ms. Carson's class." I was desperate to believe it. Instead, I focused on writing my check. Finally, in a voice that sounded more like a whisper: "She died in a car accident three and a half weeks ago," and immediately regretted it when I saw the look on her face.

Am I fated to walk this earth alone? I remember you once admitted to me how hurt you were by my "extreme independence," my need for solitude. It was the night before I left for Borneo, and you said, "A part of me hopes you have a rotten time because you miss me so much." Not even my deep love for you could quench my lust for solo travel, what Dot calls my "habit of reinvention." So off I went. I never told you this, but although I did miss you, it felt so good to be alone. I needed to affirm myself, be that fearless solo adventurer, claim an identity separate from you.

Following your death, I clung to the responsibility that I had to our baby in utero. But now what? I wish you could be here to hold me up through the death of our child. You, who would be the one person to truly understand this pain. Yet I am supremely grateful that you have been spared it.

Love,
Jasmine

June 26, 1997

Aria Joony,

You would love Guatemala. There are so many kids here. Soccer is what they like best. You were supposed to start soccer team this summer. I kept your name on the registration list just in case. There are great big trees called *la ceiba* that are taller than anything in the jungle. The smaller trees often have purple fuzz on their branches that look like stretched-out Slinkys. There are also banana trees with giant leaves and red flowers. Soon I will put you on my shoulders, and you can pick one yourself.

Love you,
Mama

July 5, 1997

Dear Dottie,

In Guatemala I have developed a different relationship with the world. I feel vulnerable to it in a daily way, realizing that no matter what shelters and safeguards we humans construct, we are still prey to its forces of entropy. Perhaps this has come from being shaken by an earthquake on a few occasions in the short time I have been here. Did I mention the chain of thirty-three volcanoes that seem sanguine in their potential for destruction? I now recognize my place as a mere human subject to the continuing evolution of life, which is quite a change from my usual perspective as an oncologist charged with reversing or at least mitigating the forces of nature.

So I work the earth alongside these farmers with whom I can barely communicate, feeling small and lost in a world of memories. Curiously, I catch myself daydreaming most about Mamani Joon, the only grandparent I ever knew. You would have adored my paternal grandma. She was equal parts matriarch and maverick, healer and fairy godmother. She lived with us until I was seven, then returned to Iran, dying just as I began college. The only way I can reconcile our distance was that in her home country she was constantly cared for by those who loved and venerated her.

Each night when she put me to bed, instead of reading me a bedtime story, she would tell me a tale from her own life. Maman and Baba were not privy to her stories, so they were our special secret, providing a fantastical springboard from which I could begin to imagine Iran. I often begged my grandmother to repeat some of my favorite ones. Mamani Joon would patiently recount her narrative as if she were sharing it with me for the first time. This story is the one I have relived most while in Ixcheltenango:

> Mamani Joon was fifteen when Agha Baba, her father, brought home an unconscious man along with two gazelles upon returning from a hunting trip. The man was of the nomadic Bakhtiari people, judging from his balloon pants and tunic. He was found a few meters away from a dead horse and had a grapefruit-sized swelling on the back of his head. For three days he lay in the living room, while my grandmother helped nurse him. She took a damp cloth to his brow, cleaned the wounds on his left shoulder and leg, and tried to bring him to life by running her fingers around his temples. She washed his hair with perfumed soaps, hoping the smells would awaken him, and applied sheep fat to his lips to keep them from drying out. It was unusual in those days and even now for an adolescent girl to touch a grown man who was not her father, brother, or husband, but all assumed the nomad would die and humored my grandmother's dedication to nursing him. "I will be a *hakim,*" Mamani Joon would announce. In those days it was blasphemous for a girl to make such outrageous declarations, as only men were allowed to be doctors. On the fourth morning, the

nomad opened his eyes as my grandmother was straightening out his pillow and said: "I must be in Heaven to find myself at the side of such a radiant girl."

Now, I will tell you frankly that my grandmother was not considered beautiful by the standards of the day. She had dark, bushy eyebrows like ram horns, a hooked nose, and a tattooed dimple on her chin, but her courage and kindness shone through her eyes and must have captivated the young man. Mamani Joon instantly fell in love. In those days girls had little access to the male world, and a mere favorable glance could convince any romantic to unlatch the gates of the heart.

The man, son of a Bakhtiari chieftain, was named Tamas. He had strayed from the tribe to find a *hakim* for his sick mother. His horse tripped on the steep terrain of the Zagros Mountains, and that is all he remembered of his accident. In the fall he broke his leg, and Mamani Joon kept him company as he faced the pain of the bonesetter's visit. Tamas entertained my grandmother with his stories of sleeping under the stars in goatskin tents. She dreamed of joining the nomads in their endless journeys.

Tamas was so captivated by the charms of my grandmother that he almost forgot why he had embarked on the journey in the first place. His mother had a fever, the kind that had not subsided despite counteracting her heat with foods known to bring on coldness, various teas brewed with special herbs, countless amulets, and even pilgrimages to sacred sites. From the pouch around his neck, he traded all of his gold coins for a new horse and medicines for his ailing mother. Agha Baba built wooden crutches for him, and by the time he left, he was adept at hobbling around. As he packed the food that the cook had made for his long journey, he looked at Mamani Joon, bringing her name to his lips though he never touched her: "My dear Tahereh, you have brought me back to life with your kindness and grace. I am your servant for eternity. I would cross the world seven times on foot to have you as my wife, only if it would please you, of course."

She was bold enough to meet his gaze and said, "May God bless the path between you and your mother, and find you both healthy when you reach her, for I want nothing more in life than to have you as my husband."

"I will come for you," he said as he galloped away.

Mamani Joon was heartbroken after Tamas's departure and did not know how to broach the subject with her father. Finally, she dared: "Agha Baba, I must tell you that I love Tamas, and he wants to marry me. Will you give us your blessing?"

"No, my Tahereh Joon. I cannot. For your sake. As agreeable a fellow as he is, living like a wild nomad does not befit you and will only cause you a lifetime of hardships. Think about how much progress we have made compared to your nomadic cousins in Lorestan. They own nothing, not even the roof over their heads! Convince yourself to forget him."

She did not say another word to her father, but he noticed her sorrowful eyes and sour mouth. She sought solace from Shookoofeh the cook, though she never broached the subject with her religious mother and doubted that her siblings would understand. However, the elderly cook had deep sympathy for Mamani Joon, promising to play along with the strategy that would convince Agha Baba to change his mind.

My grandmother rolled in the dust, her hair wild and tangled. She rubbed her eyes with lemon juice until they were fiery red. She crouched behind the samovar, looking like the crazy woman who hid in the mosque. Shookoofeh ran after Agha Baba, who was working in the bazaar, and started screaming his name: "Agha Tajeri, Agha Tajeri! Come quickly! Tahereh Khanom has been struck suddenly with a strange illness. She hides in the living room, refusing to come out, making strange sounds, and looks like she is on the verge of death." Agha Baba ran after the cook, finding his deranged daughter making animal noises.

"What has come over you, my child?" he asked with fear.

My grandmother started meowing like an alley cat. Her father shook his fist into the sky. "Dear God, what evil eye has brought this upon my daughter?" He yelled for the neighbor boy to bring the doctor quickly. Shookoofeh intercepted the *hakim* outside the walls of the house and promised him my grandmother's gold bracelet if he complied with her wishes. Fortunately, he was highly susceptible to bribery and conveyed the diagnosis more convincingly than the script Mamani Joon could have written for him.

"Agha Tajeri, I do not know how to tell you this, but your daughter suffers from an acute case of lovesickness, a rare condition that strikes girls of this age when they are deprived of the one who has stolen their heart. Unless you find a way to rectify this situation, it will surely cause permanent insanity in the long run, if not death. I apologize deeply, for there is no cure other than to reunite her with her beloved."

With that advice, Agha Baba took back his words. "Tahereh Joon, I beg you. Tahereh *dokhtar,* listen to me. I will give you my full blessing to marry that Tamas if that is what you want. Just get over this lovesickness, and I will again be a happy man." At dawn the following day, as Agha Baba rose for his morning prayers (though he had not slept a wink that night), my grandmother called to him from her bedroom.

"Agha Baba, why do I feel so weak?" He hugged and kissed her with happiness.

"I dreamed that you will let me marry Tamas. Is this true?"

"Yes, my soul. All I want is your happiness and good health."

Two weeks later a white-bearded, brightly clad Bakhtiari man left three lambs for Agha Baba on his property and a message with one of his workers that the entire tribe extended their gratitude for saving the life of the chieftain's youngest son. After this offering, time stretched like an eternity. Three months passed, six months, and Mamani Joon began to worry. Many other suitors came and went. Two years later my grandmother was gaunt from persistent sadness. Agha Baba warned her: "You are almost eighteen, my dear daughter. It is getting late for marriage. Agha Talahi's son wants to marry you. He is a decent man from an excellent family. At his young age, he already owns as much land as I do. I have agreed to his family's proposal if you do not refuse." She nodded her head with defeat, accepting her fate, for she, too, believed that Tamas had forgotten her or was dead.

Forty days after the village celebrated the seven days and nights of my grandmother's wedding, a dervish sighted a Bakhtiari group riding toward the village. There was a man at the head, followed by two pairs of men and women each on their own horses, a herd of sheep, and a guard dog running behind them. It was siesta time, and Agha Baba had just awoken from his nap. As he left the courtyard to investigate the ruckus, Tamas jumped off his horse and kissed him four times on both cheeks. "Agha Joon, with four servants, horses, sheep, finely woven silk carpets, and a bag of gold coins, I come to ask you for the hand of your daughter. My mother, may she be eternally blessed by God, has made her journey to the other world after a long illness. It is our tribe's custom to mourn her death for two years before taking part in any joyous activities, including wedding proposals. I have finally come to wed your daughter."

"My dear son, may God rest the soul of your mother. I am happy to see you. Please come in and have some tea and dates after the fatigue of such a long journey. I must tell you, however, that your arrival is too late. We thought some horrible accident must have befallen you. Tahereh waited for you for more than two years, but I just gave her to another young man, because we thought you would never return." Tamas stood frozen with that news, declining the invitation to come into the house where he had been lovingly cared for, despite insistence from Agha Baba. Tamas conceded to return to the house for tea after he and his crew made a trip to the public baths, for they were filthy from the journey.

Tamas was found dangling from a nearby *banak* tree the following morning, a rope around his neck. News of his suicide spread like an outbreak of cholera, but great care was taken to spare my grandmother from the tragic story. Until one afternoon, when Mamani Joon was playing with her niece, Parvaneh. My grandmother lifted the child up to a sturdy branch of a *banak* tree, a hallmark of nearly every courtyard in the province of Khuzestan, and watched her swing her body with delight, until she tired and jumped into my grandmother's arms. "Zan Amu," said Parvaneh, addressing my grandmother as her paternal uncle's wife, "why did Maman spank me and not my brother when we tried to climb this tree last week?"

"You are younger than your brother, Parvaneh Joon, and your mother was afraid that you would hurt yourself. When I was only a bit older than you, I climbed to a bird's nest on one of the tallest branches on the *banak* tree in our yard so that I could look at its eggs, and when I finally reached it, a greenish-brown snake with a yellow belly bit me." She hissed like a snake, filling Parvaneh with gleeful fright. "I let go of the branch in terror and fell to the ground. For many moons I was forced to stay in bed because of my broken arm and leg. So you see, this harmless-looking tree has many hidden dangers in it for a child."

"For a big person too," added Parvaneh. "I heard Maman tell our neighbors that a poor Bakhtiari named Tamas had been killed by a *banak* tree, but she said it was love that killed him, not really the tree. He had come for his long-awaited bride but found that she had married someone else."

My grandmother became instantly light-headed but somehow managed to deliver her niece to the girl's mother. She unrolled her mattress and stayed in bed for days, feigning pneumonia. This time she really felt as if she had gone mad but dared not show it in front of her husband and his family. In the middle of the night, she walked into her garden to touch the *banak* tree. She bit into the bark, which helped stifle her sobs. She shook the branches within her reach. The scaly leaves resisted her rage but dropped their brown fruit in quick succession, as if offering their condolences.

My grandmother never forgave herself for marrying Babak Talahi. She was, after all, the type to hold grudges. It was not until she gave birth to her first child, my father, that she began speaking to her husband again.

Telling you this story now, I realize how inappropriate it seems for a young child. But at the time it felt perfectly normal. While Mamani Joon fiercely protected me from the world, she never spared me the details of her own truths. We were confidantes that way. Perhaps it is her stories that inspired me to become a doctor. Thinking about my grandmother's strength to go on in the face of such tragedy gives me hope and solace. As does thinking about you.

Love,
Jasmine

July 12, 1997

Dear Justin,

You would be shocked by my purchases today. I walked into the *tienda* asking for a pack of cigarettes plus two bottles of Quetzalteca Especial. Tobacco and liquor are the usual offerings to Maximón, otherwise known as San Simón, Pedro de Alvarado, or Judas, traitor to Christ. Concepción insisted that I pay him a visit to ask for a plentiful harvest. I have no recollection of your descriptions of this syncretic religion known as Costumbre, but you must have encountered it. Concepción, like many in Ixcheltenango, is a serious believer.

I congratulated myself for finding Maximón, as his whereabouts are secret and change every Day of the Dead. He was guarded by men dressed in Western clothes and cowboy hats, cigars dangling out of their mouths, fingers weighed down with gold rings. The religious brotherhood guards their saint and are said to serve as mediators between the human and spirit worlds. I paid the entrance fee and a guard welcomed me in. His front teeth were covered in gold stars.

San Simón's effigy was surrounded by offerings of food, drink, smoke, dead and dying flowers, and a rainbow of incense and candles. He was dressed much like his attendants, in a red corduroy shirt, khaki pants, black spiked cowboy boots, and leather gloves to match his cowboy hat. Additional decorations included a large gold

Nefertiti necklace, a small, red embroidered pouch for additional money collection, a black handkerchief around his neck, and gold-rimmed dark sunglasses. There was a lit cigarette in his mouth, the ash and butts of which were saved and sold for healing various ailments, according to one of his guards who sat beside me. Draped across the room were banners of the Quetzalteca Especial girl, alternating with Orange Crush signs. With one pale hand on her hip, the other raised in celebration, an open collar revealing a generous chest, the Quetzalteca girl had an inviting smile. We both looked so out of place here where only Mayans waited for blessings. Some cried; some prayed; others just sat silently.

Between cigarettes, Maximón took swigs of the liquor. One of his attendants tipped the effigy's head back and poured it down, saving the last sip for himself. A woman brought in her sick child who was not getting better. The guard stood up, took a big gulp of the woman's alcohol, and spat it on the child's head. While the child screamed, the woman embraced San Simón, begging him to cure her child, until they peeled her away. I found myself praying with her.

My self-appointed guide grabbed me by the elbow and pulled me toward the saint. "Maximón tells me that you have come for a reason. Why not ask him for the blessing that has brought you here?" I could smell the alcohol and cigarettes on his breath as I wrestled my elbow away to hand him the goods in my bag. He smiled as if he had known all along. Suddenly it seemed of critical importance to tell San Simón why I was really there.

"I need him to protect the spirit of my dead daughter," I blurted out. The attendant took my hand between his. At that moment I was willing to do anything that he asked me if it would help Aria. "Oh, and the crops," I remembered at the last minute.

"It requires much concentration for Maximón to reach the other world," he said. I would do whatever was necessary. It finally dawned on me what he meant. I slipped a twenty-quetzal note into the pouch around San Simón's neck. The chanting began. The guard instructed me to pour the liquor into the saint's mouth as he tipped back the effigy's chair. The guard motioned for me to hold out my hands, and he poured the rest of the Quetzalteca Especial into my palms and instructed me to rub my face with it. "Like holy water?" He nodded. *"Sí, sí."* As I left the darkened room, passing by tuberoses veiled in incense and cigarette smoke, I felt victorious, as if I had actually accomplished something for our girl.

After Aria's death I, too, was obsessed with offerings, with sharing pieces of her with our community. One evening, enveloped by the scent of the freesia, narcissus, and hyacinth that Aria helped me plant, I grabbed the small shears and cut flowers until there was nothing left in the garden but the bird feeder. I filled pots and plastic, vases and jars, all the containers that had been delivered to me with love and sympathy. I forgot to eat dinner, watch the evening news, or return Dottie's phone call. I took out my address book and plotted a complicated route to arrive at every household that had reached out to me. In the dark, I left bouquets at each door.

Next I forced myself through Aria's door and made a beeline for her bookshelves. I picked out her favorite books: *Goodnight Moon, Green Eggs and Ham, Make Way for Ducklings,* the Madeline series, *First Book of Sushi, Why Mommy Is a Democrat,* and *How My Body Works.* By the age of three, I almost believed she could read because she had memorized several of them. I pulled down the framed photo of Aria's kindergarten class and read the back for the names of the children in her class. Then I inscribed: "For Matthew Rutherford, Love, Aria Talahi Avery, your buddy always." I wrote this twenty-eight more times, including *Saying Goodbye* for Ms. Carson. I placed the books in a cardboard box, addressed it to Ms. Carson's class, covered it with plastic in case of rain, and delivered it outside of the green school door.

Outside Maximón's headquarters, people were milling about, perhaps waiting for an auspicious moment to ask the saint's assistance. Others joined in the business of blessings and impossible questions. A barefoot fortune-teller with a rainbow-colored head cloth, a red sash around his waist, and crow's-feet wrinkles around his eyes sat at a table. There were red and black beans neatly arranged into groups, which he would occasionally move as he whispered to the woman who sat anxiously before him. An old man stood beside a birdcage with an emaciated canary that could pick out a fortune. I wandered to the central plaza, passing through the cacophony to find a moment of silence. Into the cathedral I went.

There among the gilt-paper cutout flowers and birds, carnations shaped like hearts, and a "CHRIST IS THE WAY" banner, I felt my discomfort around organized religion creep up. I must admit to you now that your trust in the church never mitigated my association of religion with war, discrimination, and restricted rights. My parents were the kind of Muslims who followed the rules but never made a big deal out of their faith. We had a beautiful Koran in the house with fading onionskin pages of Arabic calligraphy, but it mostly sat on the bookshelf unopened. My parents never sent me to Arabic school nor did we attend mosque. We avoided pork and alcohol, regularly gave money to charities, and I occasionally saw my mother pray. I remember asking for a chador of my very own so that I could kneel beside her, but I never learned the proper protocols for Islamic prayer. When I went to school and saw that prayer was not a part of our daily activities, I lost interest.

As the mother of a dead child, it is impossible for me to believe in a just and loving supreme being. Still, I have no concrete answers. As an oncologist, I have witnessed countless deaths. I can actually feel the difference between an inhabited body and a vacant one, even when the latter continues through the motions of life with the help of lifesaving technologies. That many of my patients on the verge of death are able to control the timing of their passing, holding on until the moment they see a family member or attend an important life event, makes me revere the mysteries of life. But I am blocked in believing in a unifying force, a theory behind everything. Since Aria's death, I have wished for spiritual comfort. Thus far, only music has touched my deepest levels.

One evening I was six months pregnant and too tired to make myself dinner. I turned on *The Marriage of Figaro* for company, lay down on the couch, and contemplated a meal to feed our ravenous girl. Suddenly, you were there beside me, although we did not speak. You rubbed my pregnant abdomen and kissed all the places where our baby kicked. You stroked my hair as you spoke to our child, and I lingered on your every word. You lectured almost seriously right to my umbilicus. "When you come into the world, I want you to be like this aria we are hearing: light and playful, lifting your mama's spirits. I am no longer here to take care of your mama, so I am counting on you. Just as hopeful Cherubino sings, you, too, will blossom from all the love that is around you." Then you disappeared.

I awoke so at peace I almost expected to find you still embracing me. In the dense fog of that morning, your words to our baby recycled through my head until the message became clear. You had entered my dream to help me name our child. Music brought us together in the first place, and this Aria would forever bind us. Only now she is both nowhere and everywhere, hiding in the organ pipes of the cathedral and in the fading scent of tuberoses.

Love,
Jasmine

July 16, 1997

Dearest Child,

Last night I lit a candle to help me read, like the time we went camping in the Olympic National Park. There was no electricity. My window was open, and though the evening breeze was strong, my candle refused to blow out. I felt you all of a sudden and looked out the window. Then I saw it: the shooting star. You loved them so much. Remember that time in Kauai when we lay on the beach at night and counted them? Was that you in the skies above, Aria Joon, telling Mama that you are watching out for me? Oh, baby, everybody misses you so much, especially your mama. Taxol and Bleo are so lonely without you. Aunt Dottie is taking good care of them right now. If you only remember one thing, I hope it is this: Your mama will always love you.

July 19, 1997

Dottie, my dear,

I continue to have incessant memories of my grandmother. This morning I was sweeping my bungalow and suddenly remembered how Mamani Joon once saved my life. Perhaps it is my first memory, though it is difficult to know what parts have been influenced by family lore. I do remember that she had dressed me up that morning so that we could go out shopping in the Marina. Maman always likes to say how resistant I was about wearing those white socks with their pretty ruffles. Even then I always preferred being barefoot. But that day I did not protest, for my little black shoes were as shiny as a tap dancer's and I was proud of them. I might have shrieked a bit as Mamani Joon collected my hair into two big ponytails. I imagine women passing by us made comments about my voluminous hair as they did about Aria's. There were not so many Middle Easterners in the Bay Area in those days.

We rode the bus into the city. I sat on my grandmother's lap and loved looking down into all the cars below. I had promised Mamani Joon I would walk during our outing, as I was desperate to be a big girl who did not need her stroller. Apparently, I ran ahead of my grandmother and picked some red tulips lining the sidewalk, roots and all, to present to her as a gift. Mamani Joon then explained to me in a gentle voice that those flowers were for everybody to enjoy and they were not to be taken. I cried from the disappointment of having done the wrong thing. On our way back from window-shopping on Chestnut Street, Mamani Joon decided to take me to the Palace of Fine Arts. Originally built as part of an international exposition in 1915, the palace was really a magnificent but crumbling dome with colonnaded walkways in Greek and Roman style surrounded by a lagoon where we could watch gulls, geese, and turtles. It was Mamani Joon's favorite place in the city, perhaps because it was the only place she could imagine herself in an ancient civilization like Iran and forget that she was in a brand-new country with no comparable sense of history or culture. We had brought bread to feed the birds. Mamani Joon saw an Iranian woman wandering the grounds and began speaking to her, excited to have found a new friend who spoke her language. They sat down at the base of a towering column near the water, as I ran around them, throwing the bread.

There was a brave gull that came within a few steps of me. I decided to catch it. Of course it ran away, flying into the lagoon, paying me little attention. I was determined to reach the bird. I ran straight into the murky water. At first it was fun, like a swimming pool. But then I tripped on something in the mud and found myself facedown in the water. I was pinned down and could not get up. I was drowning. Then I felt a big splash around me. Mamani Joon had jumped in after me. She turned me upside down like a baby born blue and pounded my back as I coughed up water between my sobs. The other Iranian woman helped take off my wet clothes and wrapped me in a sweater she had brought. Then Mamani Joon took me back to Chestnut

Street and bought me new clothes. I cried for having ruined my shoes. We went to our favorite burger shop, even though Maman and Baba had instructed her not to feed me fast food. I remember how cozy and safe I felt by her side eating a soggy French fry.

I am scavenging these memories for hidden meaning. I wonder how things would have turned out if Aria's life were blessed with an involved grandmother. Mamani Joon was a critical part of my childhood. I am sure she saved my life on countless occasions. Would Aria still be here if Maman and Baba had not cut us off? Should I have tried harder to stay in touch with them despite their cruel rebuffs, for the sake of Aria? A twisted part of me wants to know if I am being punished for having raised Aria with little mention of her family ties in Iran. Is Aria's death the wrath of the Iranian gods coming down on me?

Love,
Jasmine

July 25, 1997

Dear Justin,

Concepción has sent me to see the rest of Guatemala while we wait for the maize to grow. I stopped for a day in Panajachel, that *gringolandia* as you called it, to find peace beside Lake Atitlán. Unfortunately, children selling tourist goods continuously interrupted my calm. For the most part, I shook my head politely and smiled with a look that told the kids to leave me alone. Then came a boy no more than seven years old wearing a Chicago Bulls baseball cap and selling woven bracelets. Curiously, he sat beside me even after my *"no gracias."*

"Where are you from?" he asked in perfect English.

"Guess?"

"What is your name?" he continued, this time in Spanish.

"Yaz-mín." I said it slowly so that he could pronounce it in Spanish. He was so endearing. I offered him a banana and we both ate in silence. I could almost pretend that Aria was sitting beside me on the beach. I concentrated hard to imagine what she would have been like at the age of seven. The explosion of three firecrackers interrupted my trance, a common occurrence here. I am sure this little boy, like most children in Guatemala, carried a scar of some sort from these dangerous noisemakers.

"I want a Coke," he said, after tossing his banana peel into the bushes.

"Sweetheart, it is not polite to ask for things from a stranger," I said in English as if I were talking to one of Aria's friends.

"I want a smoothie." He was not listening. "Right now." I ignored him. He started to get angry then. "I want a smoothie," he said, this time in French, then in German, Italian, and Japanese. He punched me hard in the arm. It was impossible to pretend that this aggressive child vendor had any connection to my daughter.

"Stop it," I said. He punched me again. I grabbed his hand a little too hard. "Go back to your mother," I yelled. I must have scared him, because suddenly he was a little boy again. He burst into tears and ran away. How could I bring a poor Guatemalan child to tears?

My confrontation with another child is the real story here. Paula Crane volunteered her name, and not because I asked her for it. Paula was always a little awkward around me, as if she took the doctor-lawyer rivalry to heart. The Cranes were the only neighbors on Rainier Lane who did not stop by with food or flowers. Perhaps being so close to the death of a child was too devastating for a nervous new mother. Or perhaps she just felt guilty. "Stephanie Elias came highly recommended from the minister's wife at our church," said Paula to me on the phone the only time we had spoken since February 17. She said it defensively, as if I had personally charged her with manslaughter.

I had visions of abusing my physician privilege and getting the girl's address from the school district, but it never came to that. She was a spoiled American teenager with her very own phone line, just like she had her own car. She was even listed in the phone book.

I was obsessed with Stephanie Elias. I even wrote her hate mail:

> *I do not know how I will find you, or what kind of meeting we will have, but there is no doubt that I will make you pay for this.*
>
> . . .
>
> *I will shake some reality into you. But first, I will interrogate you: Were you drinking? Were you using drugs? Why did you turn the corner so fast? Why did you hit my baby? What were her last words? Why have you not apologized? Why? Why? Why?*
>
> . . .
>
> *I have found your unimaginative tan house. I have watched the arrogant sunbeams land through your skylight. I have seen you staring stupidly into the television, pretending to do your homework. I know your bus route. I will terrorize you as you have terrorized me. I want you to die.*

Countless times I rehearsed what I would tell her upon our first meeting. I would introduce myself as the mother whose life she had destroyed. I would lecture her about the merits of driving cautiously in residential neighborhoods, and how teenagers should not be behind the wheel anyway unless they were able to take full adult responsibility for their actions.

The day I finally spoke with Stephanie Elias, I parked my car near the bottom of her hilly driveway as I usually did and watched her walk home from the school bus stop. Soon after she entered her house, I rang the doorbell. When she came to the door, I could barely meet her eyes and instead focused on the heavy baby blue eye shadow beneath her brows. I had never before seen her from such a close distance. I was surprised when she slammed the door in my face. I was not expecting that at all. It threw me off guard, made me forget what I was going to say. I actually pleaded with her to open the door until she finally complied. The house looked different from the inside. There was light gray carpeting and impressionist reprints framed in the hallway where I expected to see family photos. Stephanie shook as she sat on the black leather couch. She was tall and thin, wearing a gray turtleneck sweater and blue jeans with a hole in the knees. Greasy blond hair touched her shoulders.

The moment we established more than fleeting eye contact and she opened her mouth, I knew she was deeply sorry, that she had suffered daily since February 17 as I had. Maybe that was all I needed, a simple apology, connection, or recognition that she was a victim too. I could see that my lectures were unnecessary. Stephanie was clearly punishing herself. As she sobbed and fell apart before me, I knew that Aria, wherever she was, had forgiven her for the accident. I told her this. Stephanie cried even more upon hearing those words. I acted on instinct and held the girl as she wept, the way any mother would do when faced with an inconsolable child. Can you imagine that, Justin? Yes, I actually hugged our child's murderer. But let me tell you something. In my heart, I could not really forgive her. When I told this story to Dottie, tears streaming down her face, she said, "Well, who do you think you are Jasmine no-middle-name Talahi, Jesus H. Christ?"

In Antigua I found solitude in the ruins of Las Capuchinas. In one of the eighteen cells of the Capuchin nuns, I thought hard about the lives they adopted in the 1700s. They exchanged their dowries for the severity of the convent. They slept on wooden beds, received no visitors, and had virtually no contact with the outside world. As I sat quietly imagining myself living this sort of ascetic life, I heard a fluttering of wings. I followed the sound until I spotted the white-winged bird in the convent rafters. Could it really be a dove? Was it another hallucination fed by too much time spent in Catholic churches? Was there a message here? The bird sat immobile as if it were a sculpture.

Oh, Justin. I miss you both so much. I miss myself too, the woman I would have become with the two of you. I miss the adolescent that Aria would have become, the inevitable teenage rebellion, the young woman who would later blossom, and the children she might have had, our grandchildren. I will never be a grandmother. Hoping that the dove really was a celestial reincarnation of one of you, I called out, "Justin, Aria. Show me a sign." My ridiculous antics must have scared the poor bird because it then flew away as suddenly as it appeared.

Aria once saved the life of a young pigeon that fell out of our magnolia tree. If she had not insisted on mothering the broken-winged creature, our cats would have undoubtedly devoured it. I helped Aria make a kind of cast for the bird's wing. Every day she held the bird and sang to it. She fed the ailing creature birdseed and bread crumbs until it grew stronger. Just two weeks before her death, Aria attempted to give the pigeon a flying lesson. The bird was so well healed, that it did indeed fly away and did not return to its little cage in our garage. Aria was beside herself. It was her first lesson in loving something with all her heart, only to lose it.

Love,
Jasmine

Stephanie Elias
Creative Nonfiction Class
Final Paper
March 22, 1999
Prof. Marilyn Levine

How I Became An Adult

"Laugh, and the world laughs with you.
Weep, and you weep alone."
—Ella Wheeler Wilcox

February 17, 1997, is a day I will never forget. Not ever. That Monday, it was like my whole life changed, and there was no going back. No returning to start. It was one of those horrible days that started off on the wrong foot and just kept on getting worse. When I arrived at the school parking lot, I realized I only had eleven cents in my wallet instead of the fifty I needed to pass through the gate. By the time my best friend Jane lent me the money, I was late to zero period, where Monsieur Mason, my French teacher, gave me points off for tardiness. I have no idea why I chose that fateful day to ask Rob to the Sadie Hawkins dance, but of course he said no (he'd already said yes to Samantha the day before). In history class I discovered the moistness in my underwear was really my period starting a week early. So I had to squeeze in an unexpected trip home to change clothes before going over to babysit for Mrs. Crane.

I wasn't looking forward to the afternoon. I'd babysat for Paula Crane once before, and it hadn't exactly been the most pleasant experience. Katie, the four-month-old, was cute enough, but she could be cranky. Mrs. Crane, a lawyer who was just starting to go back to work in the afternoons, was even more high maintenance. If I didn't need the money so bad, I would've never returned to the Cranes and could've altogether avoided the disaster that was to come. But I was still paying off the Biologicals (as Jane and I called our parents) for helping me to buy my car, my very first important possession, a gorgeous sky blue Ford Maverick. My father was skeptical that I'd actually be able to pay him back.

Road Runner was a bargain I couldn't pass up. Her former owner was an old lady who'd been paralyzed from a stroke and couldn't drive anymore. I'm sure that poor woman had driven my car at a snail's pace. With me, Road Runner's engine revved up to its full potential. I could pass cars on the freeway no problem at all. Not that I was going fast the day of the dreadful accident. At least I don't think I was.

Now that I wasn't going to the dance, I wasn't so desperate for the extra cash. I thought about calling Mrs. Crane and canceling at the last minute, but then my guilt got in the way. I was so stressed out that I grabbed a beer from my trunk.

Jane's sister had gotten a couple twelve-packs for us for the dance, and we had stashed them in my car. The beer was at room temperature and basically disgusting, but I gulped it down anyway. The aftertaste was so bad that I inhaled a couple of old cookies hiding in my glove compartment. The detour home to change my bloody clothes was going to make me a few minutes late, and I could already hear the lecture that Paula Crane was going to give me—punctuality as a sign of professionalism, the first in a five-part series.

I swear I don't think I was speeding when I made my way from Rainshadow Street to Rainier Lane, but my head was halfway in the clouds. I want to be perfectly clear. I wasn't drunk or anything. I could empty at least three of those cans before feeling much. But all I remember now about turning that corner was the flash of something that ran in front of the car. Maybe it was a dog or cat. Holy shit. I didn't know if I'd hurt an animal, but it scared me enough to try to slam on the brake pedal as I attempted to swerve out of its way. Unfortunately, I freaked and hit the gas pedal instead. I saw something fly into the air before Road Runner crashed into a basketball hoop pole.

"Oh god, oh my god," I said over and over again to no one in particular. I sat frozen behind the steering wheel. My first thought was to worry about what Mrs. Crane was going to say about the damage I'd caused. I opened the glove compartment and found my proof of insurance under the cookie bag. I clutched it to my chest. At the time I didn't even notice the pain that must've been shooting out of my neck. In the shock of the accident, I'd almost forgotten about hitting the animal of some sort. "Get ahold of yourself, Stef," I said as I opened the car door. There was blood on the fender. Jesus Christ. Children were screaming. I saw them gathered around something at the other end of the cul-de-sac. Neighbors who had heard the commotion were coming out of their houses. Someone shouted: "Call 911. Now!" I ran over to the end of the cul-de-sac in what felt like slow motion. Only then I understood why everyone was screaming. I'd hit a child.

I've tried to block out what happened from this point on. The blood, the little girl's face, her weak cries between labored breaths, "Mama, Mama." For the rest of my life, I swear I'll be haunted by this scene. At first it happened in flashbacks while I was awake, and now usually only in dreams.

The paramedics arrived. "Everyone, please stand back." They were in charge now. At some point in the chaos, a police officer took me aside and asked me what happened. I don't remember exactly what I said, only that it came out between huge sobs. I managed to not say anything about the beer. The officer asked me if I was hurt. I pointed to my neck. I hadn't even realized how much pain I was in until he asked me that question. He wanted me to lie down in the grass and lay completely still until the second ambulance arrived. The paramedics were real nice to me. They asked for my phone number right then, and I swear I couldn't remember it, but in the craziness of the moment, I suddenly wished that one of them would be my date to Sadie Hawkins.

"Pretend you're a log and lie still," said the two muscular paramedics, as they rolled me over onto the stretcher and lifted me into the back of the ambulance.

"Is the girl going to be okay?" I asked, coming back to my senses.

"We sure hope so," said the young man whose name tag said he was "Billy Charles, EMT, Medic 1." "We got here real fast, and the crew is real good at saving people." I suddenly panicked, acknowledging to myself for the first time that the girl could actually die. I started to pray right then, even though I wasn't usually religious.

"Please, Lord, let this child live. I swear I'll do like anything you want me to do. Just let this child live. I'll be your servant for life, I'll be a nun, anything, just please, God, let her be okay." The cutest paramedic tried asking me about school on the way to the hospital, but I couldn't really answer him because I was completely absorbed in emergency prayer.

When we finally arrived at the hospital, they rolled me again, this time from the stretcher to the hospital gurney, one of them at my head, the other two with arms crisscrossed around my body. I lay there waiting on one side of the hallway, as doctors, nurses, and aides whizzed by into the main trauma room. I waited forever. I heard a woman yelling in a room not far away, "Stop it, you great big, giant scumbag! You're hurting me! Get your filthy paws off of me! When my lawyer hears about this, they're gonna throw you in jail. You're gonna stay there till you rot." Was she talking about me?

Another, an old lady in the gurney ahead of me, repeated "Help" for several minutes as if she were on the brink of death. When an aide finally paid attention to her, she bolted upright. "Look, sonny, I've been waiting here all day long. I need some help right this minute."

"I'm sorry, ma'am. We have a case of life-or-death in the trauma room. We'll get to you as soon as we can."

"But what about me?"

"It'll just be a little longer. How about a 7UP while you wait?"

"Make that a Sprite. I want it with ice and no diet business."

Life-or-death? Holy shit. Please don't let it be the little girl. I went back into prayer again until my silence was broken by the shouting of a short woman in a long white coat coming out of the trauma room.

"I'm so sorry, Dr. Talahi."

"Where is my baby?"

I wanted to curl up and die. I started to sweat bullets. I held my breath and hoped my heart would stop before the doctor figured out that I was the guilty one.

"Where is she?" screamed the doctor. How did she find out about me? I put the thin white blanket over my head and tried to lie still.

Dr. Talahi was ushered out of the emergency room. When I finally had the nerve to peek out from under the covers, I saw all these doctors and nurses leaving the main trauma room. Some with heads hanging down, others just shaking their heads, a few with bloodstains on their blue outfits. Finally, a young doctor who left the trauma room came to talk to me.

"Hi there, uh, Stephanie. I'm Dr. Morrison. What can I, uh, do for you?" He looked tired but was still kind of cheery. Before I could answer, he flipped through a stack of papers and read, "'Low-speed MVA. Nineteen eighty-six Maverick versus basketball pole. Restrained seventeen-year-old female driver. No AOB. Vital signs stable. Moving all extremities. Ambulatory.' Okay, kiddo, tell me where you hurt," he finally addressed me again.

"My neck, but, uh . . . ," but before I could continue, he shot another question at me. "Can you show me exactly where it hurts?"

"Excuse me, Doctor."

"Before you ask me, I have another question for you. How would you rate your pain on a scale of one to ten, ten being the worst pain you could ever imagine?"

"Look, Doctor, I don't really give a fuck about my neck." I was embarrassed to be cussing right there in front of the doctor, but I was totally freaking out. "All I want to know is what happened to the little girl."

"What do you mean?" He looked confused.

"You know, the girl I hit with my car."

"Oh," he said softly. "It was you." He seemed to look at me with disgust, the way one might look at a child molester or murderer. Oh my god. It suddenly hit me. Maybe I was like a murderer. "We couldn't save her" was all he said.

What happened after that was a big blur. Time seemed to explode. My mother came to pick me up, or maybe it was my father. The doctors gave me a brace for my neck that I was supposed to wear around for two weeks. Nothing was seriously hurt. Just a little whiplash, they said, and gave me some big blue pills to take for the pain. At some point after the police had done their investigation, Road Runner was towed to the body shop. I never wanted to see her again. I wanted her buried with the child.

Going back to school was pure hell. With the neck brace on, there was no dodging the questions in class, in the hallways, in the cafeteria. I always left out the part about the girl, though I suspected they'd heard anyway. I carried little Aria Avery inside of me at all times like the gold cross I started wearing under my shirt. Finally, when I couldn't bear the questions any longer, I took off the brace and stuffed it into my locker. I knew loads of people who had been in car accidents of their own, so the attention went away after a few days. I told Jane the whole story, and I don't know if it was a coincidence or not, but after that we began to drift apart.

I thought of Aria a thousand times a day. I found her obituary in the newspaper, and I was obsessed with knowing as much as I could about her. I wanted to donate all my babysitting money to the memorial in her name, that foundation for Iranian orphans, but I couldn't figure out a way to write a check anonymously. My parents told me to stop, that it was a morbid fascination. But it was like I just had to know everything about the life I'd taken. Aria was in kindergarten at

Lakeview Elementary, where I'd been in school so many years ago. She was the only child of the woman doctor, Dr. Jasmine Talahi, who'd started yelling that day in the emergency room. Aria's father, Justin Avery, died before she was born of a burst blood vessel in his brain. According to a letter to the editor in our neighborhood paper written by Aria's friend, Akiko Minami, Aria loved to garden and play at the beach. According to another newspaper report, Aria had died of "internal hemorrhage from trauma to her heart."

The policeman called my house to say that it was a no-fault accident and I hadn't done anything wrong, but of course I've never bought into that. Somehow, I slipped through the system. They never did end up testing me for drugs and alcohol like they usually do after such accidents. I was actually disappointed in a way. I wanted to be caught. I wanted to be sentenced to jail. It didn't seem fair that I got off scot-free, while Aria was dead. But I also didn't have the courage to turn myself in. The officer told me to pay attention to speed limits and make sure to drive on the slower side. My parents never blamed me outright, but they didn't show any interest in repairing the car. No one ever opened the trunk. My secret was sealed. But I didn't understand why I had been saved.

"Accidents happen, honey," said my mother. "You know, half of all teenage drivers get into some sort of accident in their first six months of driving. You're just unlucky. You were there at the wrong place at the wrong time. The girl jumped out in front of you, and you tried your best to get out of the way. That's all you could've done," she said with weepy eyes.

The Biologicals tried their best to comfort me, but as usual they were totally clueless.

"I know this is hard for you, Stef. It's a tragic situation. But the bottom line is that the little girl shouldn't have been playing in the street like that without any supervision. Her mother must be feeling terribly guilty about it. If it hadn't been you, it would've been someone else. It was bound to happen." My father always misses the point worse than my mother, and this was no exception. "Look, insurance companies count on people having accidents. They can have the car repaired if you want and even pay for a new basketball pole, but they'll charge us through the nose with a new premium."

Mrs. Crane called to see if my neck was going to be okay. I think she felt guilty about the whole thing. Thankfully, I never heard from her again. She didn't even mention Aria. I was supposed to babysit for the Sears kids the following Friday night. That had been arranged weeks ago, and I really couldn't get out of it. I just didn't feel up to it. I mean, if I was capable of killing a five-year-old, why should anyone trust me with their kids? I didn't even trust myself anymore.

It felt like a small miracle, but nothing bad happened that night. Mike and Paul didn't electrocute themselves or eat Lysol. I probably went a little overboard, making them sit still while they ate their carrot sticks so there would be no chance of choking on them. They didn't even bump their heads playing tag. I was on guard the entire night, watching them even while they slept.

The worst thing after that accident was getting into a car. I told the Biologicals, "NO MORE DRIVING FOR ME." Not for a long while anyway. They seemed relieved. But in any car, I relived the accident over and over again, like I was haunted by Aria's ghost or something. I held on to the car door for dear life at every turn and saw blood flash before my eyes at every stop sign. I haven't been able to drink a beer since then. My post-traumatic stress, as I later learned it was called, eventually went away, and I'm able to drive again, thank god. But my neck pain never totally disappeared and seems to get more intense whenever I'm stressed out. And I still don't touch alcohol.

About two months later, the doorbell rang when I was home alone after school. That day Mrs. Hutchinson, my art teacher, asked me if everything was okay and whether I wanted to talk. I guess I was in pretty bad shape. My grades were falling and Mrs. H had noticed. Jane told me I seemed like a different person, and she wasn't the only friend to say something. I didn't have the patience for anything anymore. I stopped babysitting altogether. I withdrew from the world. I'm surprised that I even answered the doorbell that day, but I can tell you now that it totally changed my life.

A woman stood at the doorway. I untucked my gold cross from under my turtleneck and was getting ready to use one of my smart-ass comments, like: "I already have all the Jehovah's Witness literature I need, thank you very much." Or my other favorite: "God doesn't need a campaign manager!" But then the woman addressed me by name.

"I'm sorry to bother you," she said. "Are you Stephanie Elias?"

I was about to deny my identity and pretend to be the house cleaner, but something made me confess.

"Hi, Stephanie. My name is Jasmine Talahi. I don't know if my name rings a bell for you or not . . ." Holy shit, holy shit. I felt like the wind had been knocked out of me. "Well, anyway," she went on, "I'm the mother of the girl who ran in front of your car on February 17." She said it with a flat voice, in one single breath, without any hate in her eyes, as if she'd practiced it a thousand times. I slammed the door shut in front of her face. I couldn't help it. It was pure reflex. Oh my god. Oh my god. Aria's mother had finally found me. She knew the truth. She knew I was to blame. The one person in the world I hoped I would never, ever have to face. I stood behind the door, ready to put the biggest chair we had in front of it, in case she tried to barge in. Like I said, I was freaked out and not exactly thinking straight. I was in survival mode. I planned to call 911, but at the moment I couldn't budge.

"Stephanie, please open the door. I haven't come to hurt you. I just want to talk to you. It's important," she said, and then her voice dropped, and I imagined her lips quivering. "For both of us." Slowly and cautiously, I opened the door.

"Come on in," I managed, but couldn't keep my eyes off our stupid doormat ("Welcome to the Elias House!" it reads). "I'm awfully sorry I shut the door in your face." I know it sounded lame, but I was practically frozen with fear. What I really wanted to say was how sorry I was for everything. For being the one who'd turned the corner. For drinking the beer. For not paying more attention while I was driving. For hitting the gas pedal instead of the brake. For taking the life of her child, her only child. For not going to the memorial service. For sending the roses and condolence card to Dr. Talahi's office and signing it "Anonymous."

On the way to the living room, I offered her a cup of tea. I was desperate to get away from her, even though I realized later she was my key to getting over this nightmare. The doctor shook her head. I sat down on the couch next to her, still without looking at her in the eye. And then it came out. In gushes of tears.

"I'm usually a careful driver. I swear it. I've, like, never gotten a ticket or anything. Like, not even a parking ticket. I got a 98 percent on the driver's test. Your daughter, she just jumped out of nowhere. I tried to miss her. Honestly, I really tried." I let out a sob.

Aria's mother reached out and brought my head to her shoulder, rubbing my back as I wailed, comforting me in a way the Biologicals never could. "It's all right, honey. It's all right. I believe you."

"I think about your little girl all the time. I have dreams about her. Imagining what she was like. What her favorite color was. If she had any pets. What she liked to eat for breakfast. What she would be doing this very minute if I had been a few seconds earlier or a few seconds later."

"Poor baby," said Aria's mom, and she sounded like she really meant it. "Aria forgives you, Stephanie, I know she does.

And I do too." I cried even harder when she said that and almost choked on my own saliva.

"Really?" I asked. I couldn't believe it.

She nodded her head. Then she said, "Do you want to hear a story about her?"

I nodded, sniffling, as she wiped away the tears in her own eyes.

"One day last summer, we were out in the garden. I was weeding the rosebushes, and Aria was playing with the mushrooms that I'd thrown into the weed pile. I heard a little thump in the bushes but thought nothing of it. Probably a little chipmunk. Then I heard, 'Mama, Mama, come here quick!' In her arms was a fat little gray bird that looked a little stunned because it wasn't moving much. It was a pigeon. 'Bad, Taxol,' she said to our cat. 'Mama, Taxol was gonna eat this baby bird, but I saved it,' she said proudly.

"It looked like the bird had a broken wing. It probably fell out of the magnolia tree when our cat had chased it. We made a little cage for it in the garage. I helped Aria put on a makeshift cast for its wing. Aria fed the bird herself every single day. A few months later, she said to me, 'Mama, I wanna teach our pigeon to fly.' The cast was long gone at that point. Aria took the bird out of its cage, held it in her hands, and started lecturing. 'Okay, birdie. This is what you do.' She climbed onto a tree stump to demonstrate. 'Hold your wings straight out, flap them like crazy, and then jump,' she said as she jumped from that trunk. The pigeon was still between her hands. 'One for the money, two for the show, three to get ready, and fo-ur to-oo go!' And she threw the bird into the air. It flew, at first a little awkwardly, but then finally with grace. Its wing was all better. Aria had saved it.

"Okay, birdie, time to come back,' Aria called to her pigeon as it flew from one branch to another and then disappeared. My little girl didn't realize that once she taught the bird to fly, it would be on its own. She cried and cried. 'Come back, come back.' I had to resort to offering her an ice-cream sundae, with bananas and hot fudge, the whole works, to make her stop. 'My birdie's gonna come back some day,' she said as she ate the maraschino cherry. 'Maybe she will,' I said, trying to sound hopeful but also not wanting to be too unrealistic. And sure enough she did. Just last week. I spotted a bird nest on the edge of our roof and then saw our pigeon flying to it. I also saw three black pairs of eyes peeping out beneath her wing. So you see, Aria was right after all. I can't help thinking that even though she isn't with us, somehow she knows her pigeon came back."

We sat in silence for a few minutes. Our eyes were kind of locked together like they were stuck with Super Glue. We knew that for whatever reason, our lives had, like, crossed paths on this planet. Finally, I said, "I wish I could've known Aria. I would've sure loved to babysit for you instead of bossy Mrs. Crane." It was a mean thing to say about Mrs. Crane, but we both burst out laughing.

"Thank you so, so much," I told Aria's mother as I led her to the door. At last I had a nice memory of Aria instead of the bloody face and weak cries. "Thank you. I'm so sorry for shutting the door in your face." Dr. Jasmine Talahi got a bit formal on me again and offered her hand as she left, but I hugged her so tightly, I almost knocked her over.

"Be well, Stephanie, and don't blame yourself. Any one of us could die tomorrow, honey. Don't dwell on your regrets. It's a waste of life." With that, she squeezed me an extra time and then walked out the door.

The Biologicals pulled into the driveway as Aria's mother walked down it. "Who was that?" said my father. How to explain that the mother of the girl I'd killed had come here to me to comfort me? How to talk about Aria's bird and the flying lesson? How to make my parents understand that lightness had suddenly joined the sorrow, making my pain somehow bearable? The Biologicals would never believe my story. They would never understand.

"Oh, just some lady from the Multiple Sclerosis Society seeing if we wanted to donate money."

"Oh, good," said my mother. "I'm glad we weren't here."

That day I finally knew that I was an adult.

There was no turning back.

CHAPTER II

February 26, 1997

Dear Dottie,

It started with the pomegranate. You and Alex were grocery shopping for me. It was the first time I was alone since the accident. I told you I wanted to stay home to start responding to the stack of condolence cards. The truth was that I could not bear to face anyone. I mean, how to answer a simple, neighborly question like "How are you?" Worst of all, I could not stand another hug from a near stranger. It would surely put me over the edge.

I sat in the library barely tolerating my own presence. I stared vacantly at the piles of written sympathy. Day +9. I picked up a card with a winged baby on the cover and read the inside. It was from my secretary, Barb. It said in gold letters: "May you find comfort in knowing that your angel rests in the hands of God." She had inscribed below: "Dear Jasmine, May you find peace in the Lord. We are all thinking about you. Love, Barb." I dropped the card onto the floor in disgust.

I walked to the stereo, turning to Chopin for comfort as I had when Aria was born. Halfheartedly, I pushed the play button on the remote control: Nocturne in C Minor, Opus

48, No. 1 had rescued me from gloom in the past. You and Chopin were my faithful companions in the days after Justin's death, but now I felt nothing. You would call it emotional anesthesia. Then I remembered that Frédéric Chopin, like my Aria and Justin, was another magnificent soul plucked too early from life. I stopped the music.

I picked up the newspaper and halfheartedly searched for Alex's latest contribution, but I could not focus. A basket of clementines and pomegranates, a condolence gift, sat on the table untouched. Its bold and bright fruit seemed arrogantly colorful in the midst of the muted light of a Seattle winter. The strangest thing happened next: My left thigh started to shake like a Parkinsonian tremor. Then it spread to my right side. I picked up the fattest pomegranate and massaged its sandpaper skin. It was the color of deoxygenated blood, the venous return of an IV every medical student knows so well. I remembered Mamani Joon's skilled hands squashing the pregnant seeds of the fruit when I was a little girl. Her nails were tobacco stained and her fingers were knobby with arthritis that she made me believe were jewels beneath her skin. My grandmother taught me to puncture the tough, bitter shell of the fruit with a small bite, and to suck the juice of its maroon pearls from the newly created wound.

It had been years since I last held a pomegranate in my hands. I passed them wistfully in farmers markets or in gourmet grocery stores but had never actually palpated one since my childhood, as if the tactile experience would somehow bring back the memory of my grandmother's departure and subsequent absence from my life, remind me that my parents had abandoned me too. I kissed the pomegranate before I started to crush the seeds between my fingers. This seemed to distract me momentarily, but it did not stop the shaking. In fact, the trembling reached my abdomen, bringing up a sour taste in my throat that marked the beginning of vomit. I knew I was somatasizing again, but it did not help to bring down my racing heartbeat, the sense of impending doom. I began pummeling the fruit for the child who would never taste it, and that is when it came out.

I screamed as if I were witnessing a murder. I could not stop. I had a patient tell me once that she released her anger and fear by screaming at the top of her lungs in her car with the windows rolled up. I should have followed her advice. The rage moved from my vocal cords to my arms. I pelted the fireplace with the now-pulverized pomegranate. I grabbed the next one and hurled it even harder. Again and again, I watched with perverse delight as pomegranate blood stained the wood. Sacrificial virgins. Everything was fair game now. I split open each perfect clementine. I ripped every page of my favorite coffee-table book on Prague. I fell to the ground, deliberately hard, and began to beat the oak floor with my fists. By the time I reached the tie-dyed candle you made me in Aria's creative arts camp, there was no stopping me. I flung your candle so hard that the purple and blue wax split into a million pieces. I saw Taxol and Bleo hiding in a corner. Stupid cats. You do not even know she is gone. I rolled around the floor. I laughed so hard that I actually urinated on myself. Instead of being horrified, I howled with more hysterical laughter and then called out Aria's name so many times I started to lose it. The last destroyed object was my Waterford crystal bowl filled with vanilla potpourri, a present from Justin's mother. It made an impressive sound as it shattered. I laughed at the dead silence that followed. What an idiotic way to describe quiet. I heard my breath inhaling and exhaling. I thought about dying. I wanted to be dead even though this was the most alive I had felt since February 17. Eleanor McGovern interrupted my reverie. "Oh dear god!" she said. She had entered my house with a police officer by her side.

"I heard loud noises in here and was worried that something just awful was happening, so when you didn't answer the door, I used my key to get in," she said, her eyes full of apology.

"Well, what exactly happened?" asked the officer with more curiosity than concern. You can see how difficult it would be to explain all this.

"Officer, she's a little beside herself. Her daughter just passed away. I hope it is okay to say that, Dr. Talahi." Good old Eleanor. She tried to cover up my insanity even when she was the one to call in the cops. Once he realized that I was a physician, the officer seemed reassured enough to leave, although I am not sure why. We are often the worst at seeking help when it is necessary.

The officer gave me his condolences as if this were the thousandth time he had said such a thing. I gave them both a little salute, apologized about the disturbance, and ushered them out the door.

Then a panic to do as much damage control as possible before the two of you returned. I was mortified by my violent outburst. How could I, someone who had never expressed herself in a tantrum, lash out at such beloved objects in my library? When Justin once suggested on the second anniversary of our meeting to toss our champagne flutes into the fire in one bold, synchronized motion, I had refused. I saw no pleasure or even ritualistic satisfaction in destruction.

So now you know why your candle no longer lives on my coffee table, and why I kept you and Alex out of the library that day. I was too ashamed to tell you the truth in person, though I feared that Eleanor would tell you the story the next time you ran into each other.

I am terrified by all this rage and violence, my unpredictable emotions. Writing letters is an old trick from my childhood that helps calm me down. Will you forgive me for willfully destroying your special candle? Maybe it will help to think about it as playing a role in catalyzing my first laugh since February 17.

Love,
Jazz

EXCERPTS FROM

A Small Medium at Large: Clairvoyant Dwarfs and Other Stories

By Dorothy Wilkins

They tell me I was born laughing. I didn't actually talk until I was four, but those gurgly, giggly sounds won over even the most critical folk in Pierce, North Carolina. Those who had privately wondered if I was a grotesque came away saying, "Well, what an angel!" I must've figured out early on that making people laugh was the best way to disarm them. This is important when you're a freak whose mere appearance invites all kinds of random acts of meanness. I stand three feet eleven inches; in my more expansive moods, I'll tell you that I'm four feet tall.

My parents, Belle and Teddy Wilkins, didn't notice anything obviously wrong with me when I was born. Perhaps my head was a little bigger than normal and there was that unusual space between my third and fourth fingers, but they didn't worry much about it until our hometown pediatrician broke the news. After a series of X-rays, he informed my wide-eyed parents (some say excitedly; after all, this was a rare case for Pierce) that little Dorothy would never be normal. The doctor might have used the medicalese word of achondroplasia in his description of my condition, but then again, maybe he just said dwarf.

Belle didn't worry when I didn't sit up until I was fourteen months old or walk until I was a full three years old, but when at age four I still hadn't talked, she was deeply concerned. "There's too much twinkle in her eyes, Teddy. I can tell she's taking in every detail of the world. I swear on a stack of King James Bibles that my child is not slow in the head." My mother took me to doctor after doctor, until finally an ear specialist in Durham put tiny tubes in my tiny ears. "Ma'am, she's got an ear-drainage problem. It looks here like she may've had, since birth, middle-ear infections that have interfered with her hearing of the English language. If she's not retarded, she should start speaking within a couple months."

Sure enough, within two weeks I was babbling. Some say I've been trying to catch up ever since. Other developmental milestones were handled in creative ways. When I was potty-trained, my father, a carpenter and a practical man, made me a "magic wand" with a hook on it so I could reach the toilet paper. My teeth were crooked for the tooth fairy, but no one in town much cared about straight teeth anyway.

Thank the goddess for my stubby but nimble fingers. I was a star at the 4-H fairs (everything from crochet to baking) even in elementary school. I also won a certain respect among the kids at school for my body tricks. If they weren't impressed by my demonstrations of double-jointedness, I wowed them with fingers that could bend all the way back to my wrist. Even then I had a swayback and bowed legs, making me waddle like a duck (I was one way back for Halloween), but let me tell you something, I could run you over if I put my mind to it. I was president of our debate club, our commencement speaker, and even homecoming queen. Gotcha! I was just kidding on the last item there. Actually, I was too much of a tomboy to wear a pink frilly dress. Besides, at the time I didn't have the guts to go through all that orthodontic work to ensure a sparkling, straight-toothed debutante smile.

Nevertheless, in Pierce I had just about as normal of an upbringing as any other kid. But the minute I stepped outside of my own sheltered environment, I was made to feel like an anomaly. I remember crying once when we went to visit my grandma in Greensboro because I couldn't reach the dishes on the kitchen counters. Imagine that! Thankfully, my wits have grown quite a bit since then. That plus this damn arthritis in my back, hips, and knees allow me to splurge on Celia, the goddess of housecleaning, every couple of weeks. But back then I was determined to be like every other kid and was devastated by simple things like not being able to do the dinner dishes. In our home my dad made footstools from a fallen oak tree in our yard, and I could reach just about everything. For my eighteenth birthday and high school graduation, my parents bought me a shiny red Buick LeSabre and made extensions that lifted the foot pedals so that I could reach them. Riding around in that giant car, I was so big and powerful, I almost forgot I was the size of a third grader.

Before I started college at Cal, I didn't think there was anything I couldn't do. I figured Berkeley would be the combination of the big exciting world plus a tolerant place that might embrace an unusual person such as myself. Well, I'm sorry to say it was a rude awakening, at least at first. My roommate in the dorms, a sniveling idiot from Orange County, petitioned for a "normal college living experience" so many times that eventually I was awarded my own single room. Though it was a luxury to have so much space to myself as a freshman, I felt cheated of a roommate, hateful as she was. I once got an invitation to a fraternity party by someone I thought was a nice boy in my chemistry class only to be tossed in the air by his fellow brothers when they were too drunk to remember human decency. One of them yelled, "What does the freakazoid have between her legs?" I'll have you know I had a very nice pair of panties on, thank you very much! Another said, "I dunno. Why don't you find out?" Meanwhile, most of the feckless sorority girls stood by watching, saying nothing. Except for another student from my chemistry class, one Jasmine Talahi.

Jasmine is an AP, an average-sized person, though she is not that much taller than me. She always teases me about her extra eleven inches. That night she was fiercer than a rottweiler in heat. She demanded with all the authority in the world that the boys put me down that instant. Fortunately, they obeyed. She and I had never spoken before that night. Frankly, I was surprised that she spoke up at all. She was one of those quiet Middle Eastern girls who sat near the front of the lecture hall and looked like she was concentrating on every word the professor said, as if her life depended on it. I remember way back then admiring her thick jet-black hair and her serious chocolate eyes. We didn't have people that exotic looking in Pierce, and I was mesmerized by her darkness. Jasmine ended up walking me home that night. It turned out she wasn't the prissy type I'd imagined her to be, and, in fact, she lived in the dorm next to mine. We decided to have brunch the next morning, a Sunday tradition we continued for years later. We became best friends shortly (ha-ha) thereafter.

Chemistry wasn't my forte, and I ended up majoring in communications, eventually finding a niche among the DJs at the college radio station. They got a kick out of my booming voice and sharp sense of humor. By then I was almost forty-seven inches and sat on a couple Alameda County telephone books to reach the microphone. My big break came when Dr. Ed, our on-air animal doctor, had a bad case of laryngitis while I happened to be hanging around at the station. I grabbed the microphone and surprised all those unsuspecting pet owners. "Is your cat your only companion in bed these days because your husband never comes home? Has your son stopped feeding Fido because he's too stoned to do anything productive? Have you lost your job because you can't stop crying at your desk ever since your parrot has died? It's obvious that you care about your pets, but who cares about you? No problem is too big for the Little Radio Therapist. Call Dot for help, pet-related and otherwise."

As a kid, between being a lonely only and a glitch in human development, I had quickly figured out that animals were my best friends and had talked my folks into letting me adopt a new pet every year on my birthday. Poor Belle complained that our house had transformed into a petting zoo meets animal shelter. But it was thanks to my knowledge of and love for animals that I became a local celebrity.

Jasmine convinced me to have a couple teeth removed and suffer through braces. After all, I could've been discovered by a talent scout in TV or film and needed the winning smile. On my twentieth birthday, Jasmine surprised me with a party at the station. Everyone had chipped in to buy me a custom-made bar stool with a golden cushion to support my back and a foot stand to prevent my toes from dangling. I remember that night as one of the best in my life. After a difficult start, I ended up with an incredibly loving community at Berkeley.

Folks in the East Bay loved my radio show so much that I was given a full-time job at San Francisco's KQED. You see, in those days therapy wasn't quite so in and people were hungry for empathy and advice. Jasmine and I'd graduated from Cal by then and shared an apartment in the Inner Sunset, which worked out perfectly for Jazz, who was a med student at UCSF.

"Tell me again how fertilization occurs," I would beg Jasmine like a child anxious to hear the same bedtime story. I liked to understand everything from its foundation, from the very beginning of time. Despite my less than laudable grades in the science courses at Berkeley, I loved the details of human biology. Lucky for Jasmine, I relished medical minutiae and hospital shoptalk. During those grueling years of residency, Jasmine could talk of nothing else, as her whole life seemed to revolve around medicine. Jasmine would humor me, tired as she was from being on call, by answering my questions in a mock-professorial tone. I actually still get goose bumps hearing Jasmine explain complicated human physiology, although by now I should practically have an honorary degree in biology for all that I've learned.

My physiologic inquiries soon turned inward and focused on my condition. Jasmine took it upon herself to research achondroplasia in the medical literature as they hardly teach anything about it in med school. I convinced her that we should take our dog and pony show on the road. Of course we were highly informative and entertaining, and would have won the medical Academy Award if they gave one for community service. We took our presentation to medical schools, college genetics courses, school assemblies, and even to the city council for a forum on construction concerns for the disabled in public spaces.

"Achondroplasia or common dwarfism is a single gene disorder thought to occur in one in fifteen to twenty-five thousand people of all races and sexes. It is the most prevalent skeletal dysplasia, but there are over two hundred other such syndromes. The gene is inherited in a classically autosomal dominant pattern, with 75 percent of cases thought to be new mutations. Double dominants are generally a lethal combination and are the only approved indication for prenatal screening of a fetus from two achondroplasts. In 1994 John Wasmuth discovered the achondroplasia mutation on chromosome 16. The gene product is fibroblast growth factor receptor 3, responsible for directing cartilage development. Without that signal, there is proximal shortening of the long bones, leading to disproportionate short stature."

Jasmine had such poise and power. I never did understand why she didn't have a hundred boyfriends. In fact, there were times when I dated even more than she did. It always took my breath away to hear Jasmine speak, even though I could soon predict every word that would come out of her mouth. Sometimes I was so wrapped up in entertaining myself with my Jasmine lip sync backstage, that I missed my cue to enter the room. I typically paraded into the lecture hall dressed in a light blue hospital johnny. "Dorothy is average height for an achondroplast, which is about four feet tall. Her bowed legs could be corrected with tibial osteotomies. We call this space between her middle and ring finger a trident hand, which is very typical of achondroplasts. You can appreciate the cramped size of the base of her skull. There is a danger, especially in early childhood, of the foramen magnum compressing the brain stem, leading to central apnea and death if action is not taken. Her square pelvis and small sacrosciatic notch, seen best here in her radiographs, could eventually cause lumbosacral spinal stenosis with compression of the spinal cord or nerve roots, for which surgical decompression is the first-line therapy."

It's no surprise that I loved being center stage. My favorite was when we did our yearly lecture to the pediatrics residents. Such a thrill to watch them memorize my body, and I didn't mind the laying on of hands afterward one bit. The cuter the resident, the better! I was treated like a rare and prized specimen from the world of living pathophysiology. I was not only a live exhibit in these presentations, but an active educator. The material we presented had potential for provoking complex discussions. We talked about everything from coping with physical differences, the psychology of self-esteem, and how to respectfully ask questions of those with disabilities, to dicey subjects like the ethics of prenatal screening, the aborting of achondroplasia pregnancies, and the eugenics movement. We got all kinds of questions. After the basic lecture, Jasmine let me take over.

"What exactly is the difference between a dwarf and a midget?" Someone would always ask this. I had answered this question a thousand times:

"Midgets are the cute ones. They're proportionately small, like the Munchkins in *The Wizard of Oz*. They generally have endocrine disorders, like deficiency of growth hormone. The term *midget* is now considered offensive by many, a remnant of circus acts and freak shows. Dwarfs like me have abnormalities in connective tissue development. We'd be just about normal size if you lengthened our limbs and shrunk our heads a bit."

It must've had something to do with my own congenital abnormalities, because I became obsessed with collecting obscure medical facts. In exchange for back massages, where I would climb atop Jasmine's tense back, walk on my tiptoes, and do a few pliés, I'd demand another case report of maple syrup urine disease, testicular feminization syndrome, or flesh-eating bacteria (i.e., group A strep). It gives me such pleasure to use the medical lexicon convincingly and also brings me closer to Jasmine's world. It's like mastering an obscure foreign language. I often make excuses for dropping words like *hydrocephalus* in casual conversation, as in: "I'm so sorry to have forgotten your birthday. It must be my worsening hydrocephalus."

Jasmine, too, often weaves long words of medicalese into our conversations because she knows it pleases me. We have all kinds of inside jokes based on our lectures. When she tires of my haranguing, she retorts: "What was it I said about your foramen magnum? Oh yes, too much nerve in too little space."

We've been the tightest of friends since our college days. I survived med school, residency, and fellowship with her. But right before the time of Jasmine's surprise pregnancy, I moved to Seattle to begin grad school in archaeology at the University of Washington. I had treated Belle and Teddy with a family trip to the Greek isles for their fortieth wedding anniversary a year before. They fell in love with Greece, but I changed forever among the rubble of ancient temples. On my fourth trip to the Parthenon, I relinquished my hopes of being discovered by Hollywood and made a pledge to archaeology with a stone thrown into the Aegean Sea. Dramatic, wasn't it?

My friendship with Jasmine grew to new depths in the midst of her pregnancy with Aria. I know it'll sound like a soap opera, but believe it or not, Jasmine's boyfriend died suddenly in his sleep of a ruptured brain aneurysm (called a Berry aneurysm for the savants) while she was pregnant, a week or so before they planned to tie the knot. It's really awful just thinking about it. I convinced Jazz to leave her position at UCSF to move to Seattle so that I could be her labor coach and support her through the rest of her pregnancy, not to mention babysit. Although Jasmine seems very friendly and approachable on the outside, most people have a devil of a time trying to get to know her well, and she's never opened up to anyone the way she has to me.

Aria and I pretty much fell in love with each other at first sight. I didn't think I'd react so strongly to her as a newborn, but then again, I was a sucker for cute animals. There was something magical about our relationship from day one. I think I was the first person to actually make her smile. Whenever we got together, we would embark on various and sundry adventures that Jasmine was more than happy to let me lead since she's never been big on patience. We made bird houses with Popsicle sticks, did science experiments from ingredients found in the kitchen cabinets, and even went on mock-archaeology digs to find the chicken bones that I'd secretly buried in the garden the night before. Aria was a brilliant kid. In just a few minutes, she memorized an aria I taught her to sing from *Don Giovanni.* When Jasmine returned from the hospital that day, Aria ran up to her excitedly. "Mama, Mama, Aunt Dottie taught me how to sing me!" For weeks later she responded to the calling of her name with *"Batti, batti, o bel Masetto."*

Jasmine's parents went psycho when Justin moved in with her before putting a wedding ring on her finger. Justin's parents had an awful divorce when he was a teenager and he wanted to be super-duper sure before marrying Jasmine, but we all knew they would end up together. Jasmine's parents divorced her for good once they found out that she was knocked up and still unmarried. Of course, it was Jazz's mistake to rub it in and tell them. So, after Jasmine, I was the next closest thing to a parent in Aria's life. She was my godchild, my adopted niece, but most accurately my next of kin. It helped to have me around to balance Jasmine's demanding perfectionism. When poor little Aria cried in the car all the way to her ballet class with the strict Russian teacher, Jasmine didn't even consider letting her quit. "Aria needs to learn discipline," Jasmine told me. Well, I knew exactly how to advocate for Aria since her strict mother knew of no other style of child rearing. In her shaky handwriting, I helped Aria write: "Dear Mama, Ballet is not the right dance for me. I love the music but don't like Madame Karminsky. Can we please wait until I grow up and choose another kind of dance? Love, Aria."

I haven't told this to Jasmine yet, but I've already written my will. I need to be prepared. I'm already in my fourth decade of life, and all kinds of things can decrease the average life expectancy of an achondroplast. You know, I left everything to Aria Talahi Avery, "my surrogate daughter." For heaven's sake, I never expected to outlive my precious girl. But then came the events of February 17, 1997. I can't even bear the thought of revising my will. For the first time in my life, humor isn't helping me cope with sorrow. It'll be a long time before I'm able to have a good laugh again.

to: jazzmin@guate.net
from: dot@u.washington.edu
subject: re: bus-ted
sent: 05-04-97 11:23

Hola, Doctorola!

Guatemala sounds like my kind of place. For one, the buses are made for me, and two, the Mayans are just about my size. I once fantasized about tracking down the Pygmies whose dances are detailed in Egyptian ruins, but now I think I'll try to finagle a project in the Guatemalan ruins of Tikal. Plus, it sounds like Guatemalans don't attach any guilt to constant snacking. What a bonus.

You're not going to believe this, but while you've been gone, I've actually started aerobics. No, I haven't bought into your *Hips, Buns, and Thighs* torture, though as we both know, I could use some help in that department. Now there's something for people my size. I learned this from the Little People of America Web site. Don't laugh, because it's called the *Little Body Workout,* and the best thing about it is that the star is a glam achon just like moi. The exercises help me with the pain in my lower back, and maybe they'll even get me slim and trim. I'm working up my courage to attend the LPA Convention in Atlanta this year. I'm hoping my sexy new calves will help me get through the dating frenzy.

Jasmine, you should know that Alex looks terrible, like the incarnation of death. He's lost so much weight, and he was no fatter than a cornstalk to start with. I wish that my sadness would translate into a slimmer me. Why does it always seem like the thin get thinner and the chunky get chunkier during times like these? But seriously, Jazz, the poor boy could use a little loving from you. Call it a charity case, volunteer work, however you need to frame it to appeal to your altruistic soul. You know how I don't like to interfere. Wait a minute. Who am I kidding? Of course you know it's my expertise, especially when it comes to the life of my best friend. Please write to him, even a lousy postcard. Think of it as sparing him a few extra hours of my doting.

I don't know which is worse, worrying about Alex or the status of my thesis. I mean, who really gives a damn about the heightened (ha-ha) social position of dwarfs in the ancient Egyptian Empire? Some of their strategies for climbing from outcast to upper class are generalizable to other ancient societies and maybe even have some relevance to modern life. I cling to this notion while questioning the importance of documenting that tiny little achondroplast hands were better for manipulating gold and jewels for the pharaohs or that they were artisan gods. Who really cares that there were little doors to the other world made for their size or that dwarf kings existed who specialized in everything from frolic and pleasure to being chief of the royal wardrobe? Does it change anything that little people like myself were viewed as clairvoyant deities with important roles in magic and religion all the way back to the Old Kingdom of Egyptian history? At times like these, it feels self-indulgent to do this work. Who's really going to benefit from all this? Some other good-for-nothing dusty academic who believes that understanding the material culture of humankind will somehow advance the world? Or some pathetic soul who spends hours logged on to LPA chat rooms? I should've stuck to pop psychology or at least something more contemporary in sociocultural anthropology. Archaeology is a fun hobby but a stupid career choice for someone who wants to be of direct service to the world.

Okay, I should catch you up on some stuff that has been happening here. Your colleagues keep calling, asking me how you're doing and when you're planning to come back. They say that they can cover your patients for a little while longer, but they're going to need to hire someone new to take over if you don't show up soon. I keep trying to fudge for you, but, Jasmine, I don't know, it looks like you could lose your job. Not that you couldn't get one in a snap when you come back.

What else? I've paid off all of your bills. There was an unexpected one from the emergency room. God was it hard to see that one. I called up your insurance company right away and yelled at them, so they better take care of it. You have loads of letters from people like Frances Carson, the Gregorys, Sue Smith, Akiko and her mother, and even Stephanie Elias. I can send them to you in one big batch if you'd like. I've stopped the newspaper but don't know if you still want to receive all those medical journals. They never seem to stop coming. I've been weeding the garden. The roses are the best they've ever been. Taxol and Bleo miss you, but I faithfully snuggle with them. God knows, no one else has been in bed with me lately.

Don't be so hard on yourself, kiddo. Just because you've been a know-it-all doc all your life doesn't mean you're going to have all the answers now. You can't expect yourself to just snap out of your grief. A part of me knew you weren't coming back so soon after Arizona. It didn't quite occur to me that you'd go to Guatemala, but then again, it makes so much sense to be in a place where you feel close to Justin. Maybe you can find some closure with him too. There's no deadline here, sweetie. I miss you like crazy and am trying to be patient with your need to travel, even if it's ripping my heart out to be so far away from you now of all times. Listen, if your journeys don't bring you the kind of comfort you're seeking, please come home stat. We don't even have to tell the hospital that you're back.

Love you always,
Dot

P.S. Something to make you chuckle, a new joke I've written while procrastinating on my thesis: What do you call a clairvoyant dwarf who's just broken out of prison? A small medium at large.

to: dot@u.washington.edu
from: jazzmin@guate.net
subject: a hike to the door of Heaven
sent: 06-12-97 11:06

Dearest Dottie,

I snuck out of Ixcheltenango for some communication with the outside world. It seems my letters take weeks to arrive, and suddenly I had a yearning for your deep, sexy voice. I got on the bus for two hours to Quetzaltenango and found myself an international calling center. If you hear a voice-mail message from far away, intermingled with the operator's voice in Spanish and then my heavy breathing, it is not a crank call. No, it was me. Spoken words transmit so much more than the information shared.

Well, I did have the chance to hear your voice, only it was not as I expected. A part of me was happy for a mere recording. However, when it came time to leave you a message, I choked. Not only because I did not know what to say to you, but also because I realized that it was no longer Aria telling me that "Nobody is home right now." I remember so vividly the afternoon the two of you spent making up new greetings for my voice mail. First, you started with funny animal noises. Then you played with music. Finally, it was just the voice of my sweet daughter sounding so grown up. From the hospital, I sometimes called home just to hear her voice. So today, after four unanswered rings, I suddenly expected to hear Aria on the other end of the connection. Instead, it was your new recorded message. Trying to come to terms with the disappearance of Aria's voice in a matter of seconds froze the words in my throat.

Please understand that I am not in the least bit angry. I would have done things no differently had I been in your position. In fact, you probably should have rerecorded my outgoing message immediately after her accident. But I must admit I am glad you waited until I left.

I called to finally tell you the details of what happened that last night with Alexander. You probably know his version by now, and I certainly owe you an explanation. I can only imagine what you think of me, but maybe my side of the story will help you understand.

The night started with a datelike quality. Alex put so much effort into the dinner, and I must admit being impressed by his *fesenjan.* He even gave me the beautiful Persian cookbook the recipe came from, entitled *Food of Life.* I tried so hard to erase the past for our evening together and ended up giving him what I knew he needed. Unfortunately, it backfired in the worst possible way.

In the middle of the night, my sheets were drenched with sweat and I bolted out of bed. I threw on my clothes almost automatically, as I did when I was called into the hospital for an emergency. At first I did not say a word to Alexander, because how could I delicately tell him that I detested awakening beside him. Oh, Dot, I hated myself.

Making love to him for the first time since Aria's death was wrong. He was sleepy but tried to ask why I was so upset. He thought that we could start anew. Instead, I was as cold as an operating table. I finally snapped, though: "You may be the one who is capable of expressing his feelings. You attend the bereavement group and see the counselor, and yet desire can overtake your pain in an instant." Alex was quiet as he generally is with any confrontation. "How can you make love to me as if nothing has happened?" I did not wait for his answer and moved forward with my attack: "It is impossible for me to be with a man who is responsible for the death of my child." He stared right through me as if he were ignoring what I was saying, and that made me angrier. "Get out. Get the fuck out of my life." He looked at me with such devotion and helplessness, but all he could muster was a few words in his infuriating, characteristic calm. I wanted to strangle him.

"Jasmine, it is 4 A.M. Can we please talk about this at a reasonable hour?" he said. We were never on the same wavelength when we fought. I came to my senses a bit and tried to relay the message more kindly: "Alex, I need to be alone now." I walked out of the house and tore off a branch from one of the rhododendron bushes as I passed.

I will never get over the fact that he was watching Aria that hateful day, though I want to forgive him. I really do. After all, I had given her permission to play with the kids in the neighborhood in the past. She should have been perfectly fine. It was an accident. It was not his fault that a car sped around the corner at the wrong time. I can rationalize the matter until I am blue in the face, but the truth is that I will never see him without feeling the sick betrayal of that day.

I did write to Alexander after your latest urging. By now he should have received the letter. Though I urged him to forget about our relationship, I think of him often. Three days ago I hiked to Puerto Cielo, the granite peaks in the Cuchumatanes Mountains bordering Ixcheltenango. I walked through pastures full of grazing sheep, past a shepherd napping in the sun. In the tiny hamlets, men of all ages were dressed identically: red-and-white-striped trousers, white-striped shirts with intricately embroidered red collars, cowboy hats, bright wool bags. The women, too, wore traditional dress, tops with elaborate patterns tucked into navy blue skirts.

They were excited to see a *gringa* and laughed at my greetings in Mam. For a while a pack of young men followed me up the mountain. I could hear an occasional *"Mamacita Rica"* followed by peals of laughter after a brave one tried to get my attention. Far beyond the huts, I passed gnarled oaks and cypress trees that looked like Martha Graham dancers. I leaped across streams. Finally, by midafternoon, my destination: a barren cliff above tall, aromatic pine trees. In the distance I heard marimba and thought of Justin. The rays of the sun spilled across the valley as I closed my eyes and, believe it or not, I actually prayed for Alexander's well-being. I wept for both of us, for this crevasse that will always separate us.

I am so thankful for the structured rhythm of my days in Guatemala and grateful for the labor in the fields. Physical vulnerability is a daily reality here, and somehow it feels much safer than the minefields of the heart. In Guatemala I have found a few moments of peace with my knees in the soil.

If I one day return to Seattle, it will be because of you. You are my best friend and the sister I never had. For now, I must stay. There is something for me to learn in Guatemala. Like a tourist thrilled by the simple achievement of having made it on to the right bus, I feel a certain comfort in knowing that I seem to be headed in the right direction.

Love,
Mamacita Rica

P.S. *Tenango* means "place" in Nahuatl, language of Mexican Indian warriors from the 1500s and earlier. Thus, Quetzaltenango means "the place of the quetzals." They are resplendent birds (when male) with long golden-green tail feathers that have been sacred since Mayan times, symbolizing freedom and appearing on everything from Guatemalan currency to the national flag. Ixchel, I discovered upon arriving in Ixcheltenango, is a goddess of many things, among them medicine and childbirth.

to: dot@u.washington.edu
from: jazzmin@guate.net
subject: Shangri-la
sent: 07-27-97 17:54

I was hungry for the familiar sounds of Mozart after what seemed like an eternity of perky Latin music in La Flor, a courtyard café in Antigua catering to Western tourists. As I sipped my double espresso, a clean-cut redhead, an unmistakably American guy, asked: "Hey! Mind if I join ya?" I nodded. He seemed amiable enough. He introduced himself right away: Randy Gustafason, an ex-ranger from Idaho, a big teddy bear of a guy with a beer gut and a laugh that was heartier than your mama's home cooking.

"Jeez-us!" Randolph exclaimed, and the table shook as he slammed his hand down for good measure. His light-hearted spirit was almost infectious. Even you, Anthropologist Extraordinaire, would not have suspected anything besides levity from him after you heard his rodeo story. His secret for winning the bronco-bucking contest: biting the ear of the wild horse while he waved to the crowd with his free hand.

Sometimes when you are a lone traveler in a foreign country, especially at an expatriate bar or a tourist café, people tell you their life stories unsolicited. They are hungry to talk in their native languages, to share something with someone who might understand. Often they assume that because you are traveling alone, you have all the time in the world. Plus, they may never see you again. So they cut through the superficial narrative. They pass on heartfelt advice over a beer or two. I did not think too much about why Randy started spilling his guts to me. After all, he was lonely after a weeklong separation from his wife. He started off with funny stories, but by the time I finished my second espresso and he was working on his fourth beer, we started talking about the occupational hazards of work like ours, how we so quickly become hardened to what makes others cringe. This is what he told me:

"Our troops were always the first to arrive. We were on call to be anywhere in the world ASAP, by land, water, or air. It was our job to psych out the enemy. Our specialties were rapid infantry assault, night fighting, and airfield seizure. We would parachute in with our beans and our bullets, our ALICE pack, night-vision goggles, and rifles strapped to us, sometimes from dangerously low altitudes. It was thrilling. We were scared shitless. We knew we were dispensable. There were always foolhardy boys like myself waiting to volunteer. We all kept track of the killing tally. I know it sounds sick talking this way, but it was our own separate mind-set. Each dead man won himself a calling card, which in our case was an ace of spades on the chest. It said: 'The 197th Ranger Battalion has been here.' I'm not proud of any of this now, but let me tell you, I thrived in that environment. I was just a small-town kid, but by the time I was twenty-two, I was platoon sergeant.

"Then I met a girl named Heather Barnes. She was the nicest, prettiest girl I'd ever known. A smart critter too. One day she asked me if I had ever killed a man during my time as a ranger, and somehow I told her the truth. I left out the details, but still, it was enough to keep her away from me. Turns out she was a Mahayana Buddhist. She picked that up in college from a Tibetan roommate. Finally, she made a deal with me. We could be together only if I joined her meditation group at the Buddhist temple.

"I almost let her go when I heard that, but eventually I fell for the bribe. At first I just went through the motions, you know. Of course it was a total secret. If the rangers found out, I would've been dog meat. Make that dead dog meat. I know it sounds hokey and all, but after a while something really clicked. To make a long story a little shorter, time passed. Heather's summer vacation came up, and I surprised her with a trip to Tibet. We each did our own separate ten-day meditation retreats and met up at the end. My life came into clear focus during that week and a half. I decided to leave the rangers and proposed to her right inside the Jokhang Temple. She said yes.

"We had a Buddhist ceremony in Lhasa and then a church wedding for our parents. We've been working with the Peace Corps over the last two years, but soon we're heading home because Heather's going to have a baby!"

I managed to squeak out "Congratulations" and forced myself to smile when Randy told me about an encounter with a howler monkey in El Péten before he reached his real agenda: "Ma'am, can I ask you a question? You are awfully nice and all, but you look too sad to just be on vacation here. Would you mind terribly if I suggested you consider meditation in that nunnery where Heather went?" I did not say anything in response and just looked at Randolph for a good half minute or so.

The big guy twitched around for a while. "You can call me a busybody and tell me to mind my own damn business, but whatever you believe about how things work in the world, meditation gave me a new lease on life. It put everything right into perspective, you know? Pardon me if I've offended you. I don't usually talk to perfect strangers like this."

I looked at Randy, nervous as he was, and tried to project warmth into my speechlessness. I cupped his hand in mine, and without explaining anything, I simply said, "Thank you." He wrote down the name of the nunnery on a napkin and that was it.

So, Dot, your friend is on her way to Shangri-la! I wish I could tell you why dramatic Himalayan geography and hours of meditation will help me cope with Aria's death. I have no real answers. Only this thought: I am a transplant, a transnational, and an immigrant whose family legacy is by definition one of leaving the homeland for a better future. Maybe I will come to terms with my childless identity in a new place, one where detachment is a way of life.

I know how skeptical you have been of my flirtations

with Buddhism. From the beginning, you were against my relationship with Carlos. Remember how you called him the Dope in the Lotus? Besides, you more than anyone else know how unquiet my mind is. When we did those sensory-deprivation experiments at Cal for extra pocket money, you lasted less time than I did, but we were both rather pathetic. How those two hours immersed in water to my neck seemed like an eternity. All I heard was the loud chatter of the day recycling its way through my brain. I had no profound thoughts nor a deep sense of tranquillity, despite Carlos's fantastical descriptions of his experiences.

So, you are thinking, why do I go now to Tibet for the express purpose of focusing on the quiet within me? I must face myself now. Guatemala has allowed me to focus on the exterior world with its bright costumes, warm people, and busy chores of daily village life, but I am finally ready to do what I could not in the Sonoran Desert: be in solitude. To Chengdu, China, I go now, which is the closest my round-the-world ticket will take me. Between Chengdu and Lhasa, I will arrange my own travels. E-mail is unlikely to be available, so you can reach me at:

Poste Restante,
Lhasa Main Post Office,
Tibet,
China

Love,
Jasmine

to: jazzmin@guate.net
from: dot@u.washington.edu
subject: re: Shangri-la-la Land
sent: 07-28-97 10:08

Child, O my child, the sunset
burns upon the mountain
for your spirit.
What will become of me bereft
of your laughter?
Child, O my child, what will
become of us wandering in
the canyons of our lives
without the echo of you?

—Iroquois prayer
(translated by Patricia Benton)

Dr. Mamacita,

I want to get it. I really do. You've been my best friend for over twenty years, and I can usually predict what you're going to do. But I admit it, you've left me in the dust on this one. I really thought you'd be home by now. I understand that travel gives you perspective and escape from your home with its painful associations, but isn't three months long enough? Why did you expect to find answers doing agricultural work with Mayan families who can't even have a conversation with you when you have a real family here who suffers from not being able to dote on you?

And Tibet? Have you been hypnotized by the rich, repressed people of the world in those Hollywood films, who can only find liberation by kneeling before the Dalai Lama and consuming yak butter tea at high altitudes? Must I drag you away from the Carlos influence once again? Honey, tragedies should bring us closer, not send you running to some place a thousand miles away. Do you think you're the only one who's changed since Aria's death? Alex and I have also been shattered into a million pieces. We need you here too. I can't believe you've abandoned us. In the end, I didn't even have the heart to go to Atlanta for the LPA Convention. I can't imagine how you can traipse around the world in your state.

Today I found this Iroquois prayer that perfectly captured how my universe has changed since Aria's death. I wanted so much to share it with you in the moment. I'm trying my best to be patient, but I can't imagine how I'm going to get through this without you. For pete's sake, I can't even conceive of life in Seattle without you. Are you really considering not coming back?

Of course Alex is no help. He patiently awaits you, sulking and feeling sorry for himself. He's in total denial that you may never be with him again. He writes you these long, pathetic letters and tears up most of them before they ever make it to the mail, thank the goddess. You know, I've always been a big fan of the Cornstalk, but yesterday I nearly failed to restrain myself from yelling at him at the top of my lungs: "Repressed people of the world unite!"

Please, if only for my sake, get over yourself and write to him again.

Somehow, I was sure the Jasmine I know and love would come back after a few weeks. You know, honey, a big part of intimacy is sharing sorrow and leaning upon each other in times of crisis. Since long before your parents wrote you off when you decided to live in sin with Justin, we've relied upon each other as the most intimate of friends. Teddy and Belle even consider you to be their surrogate daughter. Stop rebelling and come home. Otherwise, I'll join Alex and get weepy on you. And that's not a pretty picture. Especially because my letters of longing, like Alex's brooding poetry, will be too cheesy to bear.

I love you and need you back here.

xoxo
Dot

CHAPTER III

January 5, 1997

My dearest Alexander,

I sit alone in my library this Sunday night at 9:30 P.M. thinking of you. The fire is crackling, the warm and playful sensuality of your Perú Negro CD brings extra rhythm to my pen, the cats are cuddling near my feet, and Aria is fast asleep. On this 46.5 birthday of yours, I eat a piece of ginger-chocolate mousse cake, drink a glass of tawny port, and toast you. I imagine you are warming yourself up against the biting midwestern cold with a cup of tea, maybe having a heart-to-heart with your ma in the kitchen, while your pa is watching TV, all of you oblivious to your half birthday.

Aria and I loved spending Christmas with your family. How wonderful to finally see the unending cornfields of your childhood, meet your wholesome and adoring parents, and yet imagine you as that brainy outsider with big dreams plotting your escape from the confines of Platte's modest Main Street, far past Lincoln. Aria is still talking about the thrill of riding that tractor with your father. It was so nice to witness the effort your parents make in getting to know you, even if they have no deep understanding of the kind of life you have led. How sweet that your mother has decorated your old room with your photos from Cambodia, Russia, and South Africa. Seeing your home makes me long even more for that kind of connection with my own parents. Sadly, they seem steadfast in rejecting me and their only granddaughter for my crime of embracing modernity and Western culture.

But I am not writing you this card to whine about the dysfunctional state of my familial affairs. I wanted to celebrate you for the marvelous person that you are and thank you for transforming my life. It struck me this evening, that for the first time since Justin's death, I am deeply happy. I know it has not been easy for you dating a woman with a young child, and I am so grateful to you that you feel secure enough to encourage stories about Justin in front of Aria. Your mother told me three times how horrified she was when you announced to her that you never wanted kids. To think that you volunteered to take Aria to her weekly Creative Motion class and take care of her on Monday nights when I work my late clinic is simply amazing! Your ma and I had a good laugh over that one.

Sweetheart, I love you not only because you have taken care of me when I was flattened by salmonella or have been a father figure to Aria, but for so many more reasons. Here are forty-six reasons why I adore you, in no particular order, in my first five minutes of thinking about you:

1. How your beauty radiates from the inside to your twinkling blue eyes

2. How rapidly your mind works, be it identifying a deposed leader in Somalia or a comeback comment of dry wit
3. How quiet and calm you can be while also stunningly passionate
4. For your golden heart
5. For your truffles
6. You ask insightful questions
7. And then you listen well
8. How you are an expressive, hot-blooded man in farmer-boy disguise
9. For your sublime hand massages
10. For your excellent mimicry of accents
11. Because you know Iran and I have never been there, and for volunteering to take me and Aria
12. For the way you hold me in sleep
13. For your contagious excitement or disgust when reading the *New York Times Book Review*
14. For the books you give me
15. And the music
16. For your flexibility
17. For the attentive, tender, and delicious way you make love to me
18. Because you generously engage with people from all walks of life and make them feel at home
19. For your strong, lanky body
20. For being an excellent teacher
21. For writing me beautiful letters
22. Because you believed in us from the very beginning

23. For the way you support your friends and family
24. For your good spirit, even when things deviate from your plan or preference
25. For your patience when Aria interrupts our conversations
26. For reading me poetry in multiple languages
27. For taking me to the Asian Art Museum on our second date
28. Because your photographs capture hearts, not just history
29. Because we can be silent together
30. For our fascinating conversations
31. For carrying Aria on her first hike
32. For encouraging my relationship with Dottie
33. For putting toothpaste on my toothbrush on my tired nights
34. For guessing accurately where people are from, just after a sentence or two
35. For your loyalty
36. For all your cookbooks with your annotations
37. Because you can take a good teasing
38. For being the first to successfully explain to me the rules of cricket
39. Because you know how to enjoy a good cup of chai
40. For those surprising ticklish spots on your feet and your contagious laughter
41. For rebuilding my computer desktop
42. And mopping the kitchen floor, without being asked to do either
43. For being so healthy of mind, body, and soul

44. For your openness
45. For your sweet authenticity
46. For the way you tip your head in thanks to the cars who wait while you cross the crosswalk, because you are still incredulous and grateful that cars will stop for you in the street

Happy half birthday, Alex! As an extra bonus for your half year, I will add that I love you because it was so easy to write this list and because there were so many more wonderful qualities I could have written here.

Your Jasmine

May 9, 1997

Dear Jasmine,

I'm restless for word of you, but I'm trying my best to understand. My therapist explained that your escape from Seattle is a common coping mechanism—minimizing the "blindside triggers" of Aria's death. I can totally relate to your need to depart. It's been my MO in the past too. I only hope that this rejection of our life together is temporary. Truth be told, I've started this letter a hundred times, because I haven't known what the right words are. Dot passes along your news, but of course this makes me jealous not to hear from you firsthand.

Jasmine, I can't stop thinking of our last night together. It was so good to hold you again, baby. After weeks of feeling like you couldn't stand to touch me, I thanked my lucky stars for your desire. It was like our dense fog of sadness had cleared for a moment. We were finally affirming life. Although it took me days of agonizing to figure this out, I finally know why you flipped out the next morning and ever since then. In our desperation to be close again, we forgot about your diaphragm, as if somewhere, deep in our subconscious, we were trying to make another child.

I'm sure the idea of a replacement kid is repugnant to you—you and I both know that no one will ever take the place of Aria. Were you thinking about this when you awoke that morning furious with yourself and me for being so impulsive? Did you hate me for the possibility of making you pregnant? Although pregnancy is not that likely for us at this age, it feels like a death-defying act.

Tomorrow would've been her sixth birthday, and I find myself horribly depressed about it all. Four days ago I walked along the outside of the Lakeview Elementary School fence—the one lined with blackberry bushes. It was Monday, my day to pick her up after school. I stared at her classroom. Ms. Carson was reading a book aloud to the class. I could almost imagine her there, sitting beside Akiko in the giant orange beanbag, her eyes slightly out of focus the way they are when she really wants to listen. Mrs. Jackson was taking a smoke break in the woods and saw me standing there. I didn't know quite what to say. I knew she recognized me, but suddenly she walked away as if I were invisible—and who knows, maybe I am. I can't imagine life without you and Aria.

I miss you both so much I don't know what to do with myself. Jasmine, don't let this tragic accident be the death of us too. I know you didn't want to have anything to do with me after that last night, but please don't shut me out now. I love you. I want to be with you. You shouldn't be going through this alone. Neither of us should.

Love,
Alexander

May 14, 1997

Dear Jasmine,

I'm writing to you from Paris, where *Better Homes and Gardens* has sent me for a week to cover the world's largest bonsai exhibition to date. I'm convinced that the *Tribune* folks are pumped about this freelance project because they're sick of my moping around the office. So, here I am, not out of any real desire to learn more about the Japanese art of miniature horticulture, but an attempt to feel some connection to you in your favorite city. I don't even know how to talk to you any more, or how else to prove my love. So, I'll tell you about Paris, with the hope that the magic of ancient Lutèce will make you feel something.

In the Bois de Boulogne, I saw living sculpture. "Bonsai is plant which lives in aesthetically balanced form, where many shaping techniques create treelike image from the landscapes of the mind," says five-foot-tall Hiro Omaya, famous here for his bonsai village, where bonsai fans flock from around the world. My favorite bonsai was a common juniper in *fukinagashi* or "windswept" form—the shape of a tiny tree living high on a cliff, where it constantly battles fierce winds. I thought of you, my sweet Jasmine, alone on a mountaintop, leaning into the wind without giving in to its pressure, demanding answers from the skies above.

On my walk to the Métro, I passed an old woman with platinum hair pulled tightly behind her neck, wearing your merlot lipstick, clicking and clacking her heels behind her three poodles. One of the dogs actually looked proud to leave its shit on the sidewalk. Ahead of me were two men in suits, blowing air through their lips like disgusted horses. At first I imagined they were talking about my predicament—*"C'est terrible, affreux, effolant, effrayant, insupportable . . . ,"* but then I realized they were just bitching about the Leftist party. There was a Congolese woman in traditional dress chasing two blond toddlers down a tree-lined street while yelling at them in her native tongue with words that were surely curses. I chuckled remembering Aria at that age—she gave University Daycare a run for their money too. When I finally made it to the Métro, I held the door for a woman in her twenties who was reading a book of poems as she walked, barely paying attention to the world around her. I imagine that she could've been the young Jasmine in Paris.

Miss you. Love you.
Alexander

May 17, 1997

Jasmine,

I'm terrified that I've found you here at the Rodin Museum—in the statue of *La Danaïde.* She's a naked, exposed woman folded upon herself in despair. Her defeated head falls onto her right forearm. The rest of her hides beneath a flexed, muscular back that throws into sharp relief bony shoulder blades, a thin waist, and butterfly-shaped hip bones that intersect the base of her spine. Her long hair flows like the water in the spilled jug beside her. It took me three slow turns around the sculpture to notice the jug. I memorized every sinew in her pose of graceful surrender, oblivious to the guard who crept up beside me.

"Elle vous intéresse," he stated as if it were fact, switching to English upon hearing my American accent. "Let me tell you a story then. This Danaïde is one of fifty daughters of the ancient Greek king Danaus condemned to pour water into a leaky vessel for eternity because they murdered their husbands. In Hades she's punished by continuing to live without joy and existing only for this one unfulfilled task." He moved closer to me—too close for my comfort—positioning himself as if to impart a dirty secret. "Do you see her disproportionately large feet, the tiny folds of abdominal fat, and the scant vaginal hair?" I nodded. "This tells you that a young woman posed for the statue. In fact, it was Camille Claudel! It was at the beginning of her passionate love affair with Rodin. Fifteen years together. Not bad for this old man." He snorted, took a step back, and then came

forward again. "Why do you think Rodin was so anxious to give away this work of intimate memories to the Musée du Luxembourg?" He took a deep breath to accentuate the suspense and then answered his own question. "You see, it was because he was haunted by the destruction of her life when he left her."

I thanked the guard and basically got the hell out of the museum. Something had struck a chord in me. Please tell me that you're not like this Danaïde, divorced from meaningful living and resigned to a hopeless fate. Sweetheart, I can't wait for you to return. I need to be yours again. Together, I know we can rebuild our lives. Even if you can't think about coming back to Seattle just yet, please write to me.

Je t'embrasse très fort,
Alexander

June 12, 1997

Dear Alexander,

Your letters have arrived. I picked them up at the post office today. It was jarring to see your handwriting. Suddenly, I froze. Where to go? What to do? I walked to the Parque Central with ivory knuckles from clenching the letters so tightly and sat on a white bench facing the Greek columns of the Casa de la Cultura. I read my other letters first. In the meanwhile, young boys offered me a shoe shine though I was wearing sneakers. Taxi drivers, too, advertised their services. Lone men decades younger than me gave me the look as they passed. One of them even said *"Adiós"* as if we had been conversing. I stood up, heart pounding, and walked triple the speed of most Guatemalans. I needed a private place in which to absorb your words.

I arrived at the gringo café: La Luna. I managed a *"buenas tardes"* and sat myself as far from the front counter and the smiling waiter as possible. Aside from violins playing Pachelbel's Canon in the background, the only other sounds were hushed conversations at neighboring tables. At last, some peace and quiet. I ordered an espresso to justify my existence in the café.

By now you should have received my letter of apology, so I felt slightly less guilty about the brusqueness of my departure. Still, my hands shook more than the first time I made an incision into human skin. I took a deep breath. Then I read. There was espresso on the table that must have been brought to me while I was deep into your letter, dear

Alexander, for I had no recollection of the waiter passing by. I took a quick sip and burned the roof of my mouth. Then I started to cry, silent tears at first and then big gulping sobs. My context was back. I put money on the table and fled the café.

I walked as if I knew where I was going. Then I ran. Buses belched their exhaust in my face, bicyclists nearly hit me, but nothing could stop me. I read every sign that passed like a child who first learns to make sense of letters thrown together: "BIMBO: SIEMPRE RICO Y FRESCO." "FARMACÍA FERNANDO." "BANCO OCCIDENTE." "PENSIÓN SUEÑOS DE QUETZAL." "CAFÉ CRUSH." "CANTINA CORAZÓN VIEJO." As if stuffing my brain could stop its internal processing. The sweat in my palms smeared the return address on one of the envelopes. My throat was dry and taut as if suspended in a scream. I finally stopped crying. I walked on the road, too impatient to weave my way through the maddeningly relaxed pace of the Quetzaltecos on the sidewalk.

Maybe I knew I was heading there all along. I had seen the small pastel village from high in the mountains when I first descended into the city by bus. On foot, it was immense, an entire city of the dead. I entered through the cemetery's vaulted archway, and somehow it calmed me. The graves commanded respect. Or maybe it is because I am counted among the living dead. The nicest section was the one closest to the entrance. There I found ornate mausoleums, family shrines, and sculptures suitable for the Tuilleries. There were miniature cathedrals that reminded me of Chartres, pyramids that were replicas of the ones in Giza, and a family of astronomers who were buried in a tomb shaped like an observatory.

I walked farther, beyond the steps, descending through the sharp demarcations of class. In the slums of the cemetery, graves were jammed in every which way with none of the stately respect of the opulent tombs. There were bright tombstones, occasional crosses, and fresh flowers vibrant beside wilted and dead ones. The place was dusty, with no refuge from the unyielding sun. I returned to the ritzier area and sat beneath the shade of a sphinx.

Replacement child. I am haunted by those words, by everything that you have written. How I have castigated you for Aria's death. I realize there is not a single person to blame. Why was I not at home watching Aria after school? Why were you two not cooking or reading a book together? Why did Ginny McGovern not hide Aria with her like she usually did during those games of kick the can? Why did Aria choose that moment to run toward home base? Why did Stephanie not swerve out of the way? All the whys and what-ifs recycled through my head, torturing me with different scenarios, all of them infinitely better than the one that occurred.

How can I convince you to move on with your life and forget about being with me? You deserve someone who will care for you as exquisitely as you have done for me. The day I lost Aria, a part of me died too. The Jasmine that remains is not capable of loving again. I am so sorry to disappoint you. I know much less than I did four months ago, but this much I know is true: Like the generations that come before me, I must now honor this steady longing for flight.

Love,
Jasmine

CHAPTER IV

August 7, 1997

Dear Dot,

An earwax picker, itinerant dentist (or rather, extractionist), and foot-callus remover offer me their services as I sip a bottomless cup of my namesake tea. The only one who does not stare at me in this Szechuan teahouse is the blind masseur. Few actually make verbal contact, aside for the old men wearing navy Mao jackets. They learned English in pre–Cultural Revolution days from Voice of America radio and seem genuinely pleased to speak to me. It is easy to spot them as they are often seen escorting their songbirds in lacquered bamboo cages.

Their calm is in sharp contrast to cutthroat bicycle riding in Chengdu. Bikes are the only reasonable way to get around here. On my rusty three-speed, a "Flying Pigeon," I feel as if the city's ten million inhabitants are in the lane with me. I weave around them, cursing under my breath as they cut in front of me, constantly ringing their bells. Many daredevils in high heels and miniskirts whiz by me laughing. Crashing seems imminent, especially if I am not able to dodge the hawkers, peddlers, artisans, and rickshaw drivers who have stopped paying attention to the road since they got cell phones. If I dare turn back, a sea of curious faces stares at me. They scream their singsongy "hallo, hallo" into my face or attempt to engage me in an impromptu English lesson. My shoulders and neck ache from this bicycle riding, enough to have brought me into Traditional Medicine Hospital 2 in search of Chinese massage.

After describing my symptoms at the intake counter, I was sent to the traditional Chinese medicine doctor with the best English. Dr. Fu resembled a squirrel in his energetic movements. Enormous tartar-stained front teeth barely shielded his saliva when he spoke. The arteries on each temple looked like they might explode every time he smiled. Long white hairs deviated from his nostrils, outer earlobe, and chin. After taking my pulse and looking at my tongue, he suggested acupuncture instead. He must have thought an American could not tolerate his big Chinese needles, for he suggested "finger acupuncture" or acupressure.

On an examining table, Dr. Fu dug his short but powerful fingers into my meridians. Early in the process, when I was still among the conscious, I asked him about his medical belief system. "The Buddha's Fa," he replied. He stopped the pounding of my muscles for a split second, and I could imagine a fountain of saliva hitting my back. "Buddha's Fa: universal law and principles. Truth, compassion, and forgiveness. Some doctors think treating patients good deed. My opinion is not really cure illness, but postpone karma. True healing comes from study of *falun dafa,* highest Buddha practice."

At that moment the acupressure seized hold of me. It was not physical pain, mind you, but something much deeper, like an electrical shock or the sensation of energy flowing. Tears fell swiftly from my eyes as if they alone were meant to fill the locks of the Yangtze River dams. My body barely remained on the table. It twitched with movement even after his fingers had left my body, as if Dr. Fu had accessed the meridian of feelings. I left China and was back at University Hospital. I paced the main entrance hallway like a ghost. In Seattle it was the middle of the night. I passed the espresso cart. At each piece of art, I paused, carefully inspecting the image. This was in contrast to years of rushing by and merely glancing at the walls as an afterthought. The halls were empty except for the Eritrean and Cambodian custodians, who were mopping the floors and smiled as I walked by them. I glanced down at myself and noticed my pregnant abdomen covered by a patient gown. I patted my pelvis, promising my child-to-be that I would devote my entire life to her, do everything I could possibly do to compensate for a father who had abandoned us through no fault of his own, victim to his own ticking time bomb. I made my way back up to the labor and delivery floor even though my contractions were hardly noticeable.

I met my obstetrician at the entrance to my room. "We have been waiting for you," she said sharply. She connected me to the fetal monitor. I turned to look at my baby's heart rate and saw Alexander by my side. He held my hand as if he had been there with me the whole time. "Too many decelerations," the doctor said with a worried look on her face. "We need an emergency section."

They rushed me into the operating room, and there was no time to put up a drape between my belly and face. The doctor plunged her hands into my lacerated abdomen and held up my baby, a blue umbilical cord wrapped around her neck, looking bruised and bloody, not making a sound. She handed the baby to Alexander, saying, "Congratulations on your new baby girl!" Before I was able to tell Alexander to make our baby cry, she slipped out of his hands and fell to the floor with a loud thud. I heard the pediatric ICU paged for the emergency over the loudspeaker. Before the nurse wheeled me out of the operating room, I knew that my baby was dead. She had no pulse. The pediatricians attempted a violent resuscitation with CPR and long needles into her chest, but it was to no avail. Alexander had long since stopped holding my hand. First, he leaned up against the wall, staying out of the way of the failed resuscitation. Then he backed his way out through the door and slumped to the floor.

I shook and gasped. Suddenly, I was back in Traditional Medicine Hospital 2. Had I fallen asleep or was this an acupuncture-inspired vision? There was no time to find out. I was desperate to leave. Dr. Fu seemed pleased by my reaction. "Buddha's Fa framework for man and universe. Insight. Moral guide." I jumped to my feet clumsily, ignoring my dizziness, bowed my head in thanks, and ran out of the Chinese hospital as fast as I could. I tripped in a gutter outside the clinic while onlookers paid me no heed. The pain leveled me.

As I rode my bicycle back to the hotel, I passed the bicycle police, mostly elderly women in yellow vests and matching caps. They blow their whistles and raise their red flags to stop traffic at the intersections, but they do not care about the vulnerable. The Chinese children stand on book racks with their arms wrapped around adult shoulders, heads unprotected. I found myself shouting at one of the mothers who almost crashed into me, a daughter on the handlebars and a son behind her: "Helmets, you fool! You need helmets! How can you risk your children's lives?" I shook my foreign head at her. She stared blankly at me. I imagined her response: "Stupid big nose, it is your fault. Who invited you here?"

I growl now at the slightest provocation: pollution assaulting the eyes and lungs, exponentially growing construction destroying the green spaces and historic wooden pavilions, thick phlegm evacuated from the deepest recesses of the throat and surely spreading infections, babies with slits in their pants to vacate their excrement at will, Buddhist and Taoist temples stripped of their frescoes, a disintegrating Mao statue facing huge cigarette advertisements reminding the people of empty promises, a Cultural Revolution that sent doctors to work in the fields in provinces far from their families, and an epidemic of suicide among the rural women. No one understands my ranting, least of all myself.

Had I betrayed Aria? Was I being punished for my selfishness? I knew that Alexander never wanted children, and yet I put Aria in his care. I chose a man who adored me but only tolerated my daughter. And then she died while he was responsible for her. Was it simple coincidence or karmic payback? Alex carries these preposterously romantic notions of me as a sturdy bonsai in a chic Parisian arrondissement. Tell him that I have been swept away to harsh mountainous terrain. That I am in the land of the Buddha, a man who abandoned his family to search for enlightenment. That I, too, am searching for something and need my distance.

For my last dinner in Chengdu, I ordered several skewers of spicy lotus root, perhaps for its symbolic meaning. Never before have I so badly needed the compassion of the Buddha. This anger was exhausting and I actually looked forward to sleep. Each night is another chance to reunite with Aria. Thus far, I have not been able to dream about her. Then again, perhaps I am lucky: I have also been spared from reliving her death over and over again in my nightmares.

Love,
American Bicycle Police

August 14, 1997

Tashi delek, dear Dottie!

I have finally arrived in Lhasa. If there is any place on earth you might feel tall, it would be here: "The Roof of the World!" Of course, the altitude sickness may have something to do with it. Flying from sea level to nearly twelve thousand feet can do strange things to the mind. I was beginning to think that I would never escape Chengdu. I feared I would be spinning my bicycle wheels through that Szechuan city for all of eternity like some poor unenlightened waif recycling through the phases of rebirth. Instead, at half past three in the morning, I write to you from the Land of Snows Guest House, feeling vaguely celebratory about this acute mountain insomnia.

Today I did nothing but circumambulate the Barkhor, the circuit around the Jokhang, one of the most revered Tibetan Buddhist temples. Moving in clockwise fashion, I pinched myself repeatedly to convince myself that I was not sleepwalking in centuries from the past. The pilgrims weave through the crowds, for the Barkhor is not only a sacred destination but it also is the heart of the old Tibetan part of town and the commercial district. Stalls encircle the Jokhang. This holy bazaar features everything from putrid yak butter to Vaseline, bright prayer flags to rusty monastery keys, camping gear to pirated rock-and-roll tapes, charms to children's clothes.

Amidst the prostrators are saffron-robed monks chanting in front of their alms bowls. Tibetans who have been dispersed as far as Nepal and India to the Qinghai and Gansu provinces in China have come to the Barkhor, for it is a culmination of holy merit, akin to a trip to Mecca for the Muslims. With a rosary in their left hand (often positioned at the sacrum) and a prayer wheel in the right (also moving in clockwise fashion), they repeat millions of *Om mani padme hum*s under their breath. The steady drone of this mantra comforts me somehow. I find myself mouthing the words over and over again during these holy laps, although I am sure I am missing something about its deeper meaning.

Walking is the fastest way around the Barkhor. The only use of wheels is to expedite mantras. Prostrating pilgrims have worn the stones smooth with their devotion. The wealthier ones wear wooden shields on their hands and knees. Some wear flip-flops on their hands alone. The poorest ones who wear no protection at all develop thick calluses that they display like badges of honor. Clasped hands over their foreheads then lips then hearts, they lower to their knees, touch their foreheads to the ground, diving forward, a little conch shell (a symbol of enlightenment) at their fingertips marking the limit of the next steps. It is the old women pilgrims, with deformed knees and hunched backs, who take part the most passionately. Inching their way painstakingly around the circuit for an entire day, they make me feel guilty for walking it at a relaxed pace of thirty minutes.

The hardest part for me about the Barkhor is the beggar children. Little urchins, wearing nothing but rags, they grab my leg like they do not want to let go. The last time I felt a child hold on to me this way, it was Aria as a toddler, during her short rebellion against University Daycare. The first time it happened to me, the crowds went silent. My head was so light it could have floated through the air along with the incense. Before I knew what I was doing, I lifted the Tibetan toddler into my arms and clenched her tight, walking toward my guesthouse, as if I were taking her home. Alerted by her child's terrified screams, the mother ripped her away from my arms. The disapproving looks melted only partially after I bowed my head several times and attempted the Tibetan word for *sorry,* as well as handed the woman a fist full of bills large enough to send her entire village on pilgrimage. Since then I have spent much of my energy at the Barkhor dodging the beggar children.

What is it that I seek in meditation, in traveling to this remote nunnery in the Himalayas? Will I finally understand something about the devotion of these Tibetan pilgrims? Is it possible for me to develop faith now, after everything that has happened? Or at least a kernel of wisdom? Maybe Tara, the goddess who embodies the enlightened mind of Buddhahood, will offer me guidance. Or perhaps Tara is nothing more than the sturdy web of friendship that you have created for me, the net that will catch me after I fall.

Love,
Your Favorite Wandering Soul

August 17, 1997

Dear Dot,

Two days ago I arrived at the *ani gompa,* which literally means "nun's dwelling in solitude." It was an eight-hour trip on rudimentary roads by land cruiser. We stopped to dig the path out from beneath a landslide. It was a powerful metaphor, a good omen, I think. The driver was a young man with a single red braid wrapped about his head. He wore imitation Levi's and spoke very little English. The Tibetan phrase book I found in the airport bookshop has been critical for communication. The driver's name is Tundru, which my book tells me means "one who has attained his goals." Another good sign.

BerTse Ani Gompa deserves to be called one of the holy places of the world. The modest ocher temple is surrounded by the white-walled brick courtyards of the living quarters. They sit at the base of an imposing cliff of weathered rock in a grassy valley dotted with grazing animals and carved by a windy stream. Undulating hills encircle the valley and seem to hug the four corners of the horizon. The jagged peaks of the Nyenchentanglha Mountains look like vigilant soldiers with their twin spires of over twenty thousand feet at either end of the nunnery. Every *gompa* that I have seen thus far seems to occupy a strategic military location, as if prepared for attempted desecration by the Chinese.

The nuns range in age from four to over ninety. The head abbess is a plump woman in her seventies, missing all her teeth except for a lower canine and with numerous wrinkles that make her face look like a topographic map when she smiles. When I present her with a note saying that I would like to explore Buddhism through meditation, she nods and asks no questions nor offers any advice. She shows me to my bed, a simple cot, in a room where three other nuns sleep. She invites me to share their meals. Tundru's translation skills are limited, so I never learned what the nuns' past experiences with foreigners have been. It seems clear that I will be on my own at BerTse Nunnery. The head abbess treats me with kindness but remote interest.

I can almost tolerate the yak butter tea she offers me, although I pine for the tea of China, the only thing I miss about that place. There are different grades of yak butter tea, I have learned. The trick is to drink it while it is still hot. Otherwise, the cold tea separates the residues of rancid, sour conglomerates of fat from the salty brew. The yak butter tea gives me the hydration and caloric intake that my body needs since I have decided to fast while meditating, eating only the evening meal with the nuns.

Randolph's wife, Heather, found a good cave for meditating on the cliff above the *ani gompa.* I have followed her advice and am spending my days in this cave. I still remember Carlos's insight meditation technique. It seems the simplest and most obvious choice for me as a beginning meditator not intellectually steeped in these Buddhist traditions.

From my little hermitage, I can see herds of Tibetan gazelle, sheep, and goats. I hear them baying to the world.

Shepherdesses in fluorescent pink and green head scarves tend to them with affection and sing them folk tunes as if they were children. In my view, there is a *drogpa* encampment, marked by a large brown yak-hair tent. The *drogpa* are the nomads of Tibet. Their name literally means "men of solitude." I feel solidarity with them now as I wander alone through the thick planes of tundra.

I am beginning to acclimate to the sixteen thousand feet of the *ani gompa.* My days begin with the vibrations of the temple gong just after sunrise. The *anis* and I arise shivering as the wood-burning stove has extinguished in the middle of the night. Kama Shoompy is in charge of putting a few scoopfuls of dried yak dung (our only source of fuel) in with the juniper branches (the only wood that grows at this altitude) to relight the stove. Shortly thereafter, Kama Yondrew brings me a basin of water that she has carried on her back from the stream. The water I boil for drinking and washing. I take a sponge bath, straighten up the room, do the half-hour climb up the hill to the cave.

I spend morning through late afternoon in the cave sitting in lotus position on my old sarong from Borneo. Every couple hours or so, I ring a little bell to summon my ten-year-old meditation assistant, Degi Shonam. She is usually outside, throwing rocks at the *drogpa* dogs rather than paying attention to her studies. With pride and a sense of importance, she pours the glass thermos of my daily nourishment as she has been trained to do during chapel ceremonies. At first I insisted that I could pour my own tea and did not need an attendant. But Degi Shonam refused to listen to me and gave me a look that said, "Let me do my job and I will let you do yours."

By 6 P.M. I rejoin the nuns and help with dinner preparations. Sometimes I cook the rice, make the barley porridge we mix with tea called *tsampa,* or wash the dishes. Rarely do I venture into the temple. It seems a dark and possibly sinister place, inhabited by hundreds of Buddha figurines, mandalas with monsters, and primitive-looking percussion and wind instruments. In the evenings the nuns and I alternate between staring at each other, doing sign language, and attempting simple communication via my phrase book. This socializing usually continues until nightfall, by which time I am exhausted and ready for bed.

A handful of the *anis,* your colleagues the anthropologists, I call them, usually follow me into the room where I sleep and watch with fascination as I brush my teeth. The way they handle my toiletries and other belongings, it is apparent that their contact with foreigners has been limited. They never seem to tire of sniffing the toothpaste and soap, laughing to each other before wishing me *simja nâng-gaw* (good night) and letting me sleep.

Love,
Your *ani* (in training)

August 20, 1997

Dear Justin,

I feel you close here in the soft evening light of the Himalayas. The Nyenchentanglha Mountains consume the vista like a giant reclining Buddha in the foreground. You were the one who first opened my eyes to the beauty of the natural world: You taught me to appreciate the silhouettes of raptors, the seasons in the pine tree, the vast theater of the stars. There is something so pure and simple about this, about the way you were.

The men in my life have always seemed to be searching for answers to ineffable questions. You were the exception. I loved how straightforward you were, how easily you found joy everywhere. Dot put it well: You were a romantic comedy and I, a docudrama. I miss your bedtime stories. Our wrestling matches. Those high school kids were devastated after your death. What they said about you at the memorial, "magician in the classroom." Oh, what I would give to hear your throaty laugh, watch your head rock back and forth in surrender to mirth. A perverse confession: I wear your brand of deodorant now. In Tibet it is so cold that axillary bacteria hardly survive and deodorant is unnecessary, but I wear it anyway, to feel you near.

I think I finally understand my habit of solo travel, the little fissure in our relationship that you never accepted. Dot thinks it was about a primitive need to escape my environment. But that is not it. In travel, I am intimately involved with the fundamental elements of life. Basic functions occupy my whole day: how to secure food and shelter, how to maintain health, how to communicate. In this modest migration from point A to point B, under rudimentary conditions, devoid of the safety net and expectations that accompany common language, culture, and geography, I get in touch with what it means to be human. I am a distilled version of myself. I finally become simple.

With oncology, I thought I had a taste of this too. The doctor-patient relationship was a pure sort of love. My role was well defined. I listened well. I was empathic. I knew what science had to offer, and I could predict what my patients wanted by paying close attention, before they had even verbalized it. One of my patients, a bush pilot with rectal cancer, called me Dr. Bodhisattva, "the doctor who had come back to earth to liberate the suffering." I wanted to believe what she said. What arrogance on my part. After all the time I spent with my patients, I saw myself as separate from them. That I tended so well to their suffering meant that I might be protected somehow. Even your death did not stop me from that delusion. Against all odds, you left me a part of yourself in Aria.

Darling, it is time for me to say good-bye, to accept that I will never understand why your time on earth was so abbreviated or why Aria only lived to age five. I am supremely lucky to have known you both. What hubris to think that I had figured out dying or that I understood what grief means for any individual. In my oncology practice, I actually used a generic condolence letter that I wrote as a template to send to the families of my patients when they passed away. I thought that despite the differences in each person's life, human beings were so very simple at the end. I was terribly smug in my goodness and certainty. In fact, I understood nothing.

Love,
Jasmine

c:/condolence letter/talahi/doc

Dear ________ Family,

It is with great sadness that I compose this card to you. By now, I have taken care of many wonderful patients who are ultimately consumed by their cancers. This is always a tragedy: life truncated prematurely, family and friends left behind to grieve, futures altered permanently. I take solace in knowing that ________ died gracefully, surrounded by your love and support, in minimal pain, at peace in the end, though he/she fought like a champion.

I feel privileged to have known him/her and miss him/her too. It was a gift to know ________ and you by extension. Please feel free to call anytime or make an appointment to see me if it feels like the right thing to do. Please accept this book as a token of my affection for ________. May it give you hope and guidance in the most difficult moments of your grief as it has done for many of my patients' beloveds.

Heartfelt condolences,

Jasmine Talahi, MD

August 22, 1997

Dear Dot,

Please remind me why I ever thought sitting silently for ten hours a day might be therapeutic? It has been a week now of my attempts at cross-legged meditation, and I want to run screaming out of this cave. Of course, I have limited communication with the nuns, so I have found little sympathy here. Crying does not help much. Except to make the young Degi Shonam laugh at me. My focus is fractured. I have tried to breathe in compassion, detach from selfishness, and be perfectly silent. But my concentration falters. I try to redirect my promiscuous mind back to the pathway of my breath. I even tried chanting *Om mani padme hum*s to occupy my consciousness and give order to my breathing. But my ego gets in the way. It is impossible for me to disconnect. I think about everyone in my life, alive and dead. I relive my travels and my daily life in Seattle pre-accident, recount family stories, and have inner dialogues. I write you these letters knowing full well that they will not reach you for several weeks, if not months. My mind is a Mexican jumping bean. And yet I am not quite ready to give up. I can finally sit in lotus position for hours at a stretch. Perhaps focused meditating will come with time. I know you think I am being silly and competitive, and maybe you are right, but I am desperate to do this right.

Love,
Your incompetent *ani*

September 2, 1997

Dear Dot,

I am still here. I have not yet managed to extinguish myself through concentrated breathing, but I can finally be of some use in the elements. Yours truly lights fires with animal dung in the harshest of winds and makes edible gruel from fresh barley. Oh, what the nuns have taught me: practical skills to complement the nebulous spiritual work that occupies most of my day.

Apparently, there is much more to be learned, especially when it comes to uses of the yak, the *anis'* most precious commodity. The blood can be drunk warm and fresh (an aphrodisiac like snake blood, I wonder? Bad *ani,* bad *ani*!) or conglomerated into sausage. The lungs, spleen, and stomach make useful receptacles. The hide makes excellent floor coverings and tents. The hair can be woven into sturdy rope and durable blankets, and the skull displayed on rooftops to intimidate evil spirits. Not a piece is wasted.

My most evolved talent, however, is stone throwing. You would be impressed by how good my aim is. Each day as I walk to my cave, my pockets are weighed down by little cannonballs ready to be launched at my enemy: the ferocious dogs trained to attack foreign smells. This is the ultimate low-tech security system. Degi Shonam has shown me the tricks of the trade. Once, I was so engrossed in walking that I did not spy a canine coming my way. Unfortunately, my pockets were empty. As a last-ditch effort, I bent down to hurl an imaginary stone. I like to think that based on my previously demonstrated skill, the motion scared off the salivating mutt.

Do you remember how I used to be plagued by recurring images of my own death? Though I must admit, I never thought of death by wild dog attack. Most often the mechanism was breaking my neck from a bad fall or going over a cliff in a car that had lost control of its steering wheel. You were the one who encouraged me to see a counselor. I had so many questions: Why was I having these disturbing visions and what did they mean? Was I obsessed with death? Was I having premonitions of my own death? Was this my reaction to having chosen a field where I would have to face the death of patients daily? The counselor smiled when she heard what was haunting me. She reassured me that it was a "healthy eject button," a means of escaping the intensity of my life should it become too overwhelming. "You take on so much that to continue on as you do, you need to know that you can have a disappearing act in your bag of tricks." Maybe she was wrong. Maybe I am the latest incarnation of the grim reaper.

I have recently started sitting with the nuns in their temple during the hour before we begin the dinner chores. I find their chanting to be comforting, and there is strange solace in looking at the Buddhas. In their eyes, I see a suggestion of squelched longing. Perhaps they have lost children, too, or wish they could dream about their departed loved ones. Their smiles are aloof, inward, as if they accept that happy recollections cannot be relived or even acknowledged.

The nuns, as androgynous looking as the Buddhas with their shaved heads and shapeless robes, are a different story altogether. They are full of personality and individual human flaws. Of my roommates, Kama Shoompy brags about the number of Dalai Lama photos she has acquired, Kama Yondrew becomes jealous if I sit beside anyone else at dinner, and Kama Bamoo cannot tolerate our presence when she has a headache. They were not born to be good meditators, but they have mastered the art through daily practice. I think about this as I sit in the endless silence of the cave, separated from everything of value to my life. I have been crying a lot, but it is getting easier.

Love,
Jasmine

September 8, 1997

Dear Dottie,

In my remote cave, at the edge of this valley enclosed by towering mountains, quiet pervades. Usually, it is only my brain, attempting to silence itself, that produces noise. Today as I sat in lotus position, I thought I heard chanting and the monotonous drone of trumpets. It could have been a figment of my imagination. Then it came again, this time with cymbals and kettledrums imitating thunder in the distance. Outside my cave, I heard the sounds of lamentation. The melody was one of smooth, uninterrupted distress, as if all the suffering of the world was breathed into these instruments. This was not a dream. Something had happened. Degi Shonam was nowhere to be found. I left the cave and headed for the *ani gompa.*

On the lower hilltop across from where I stood, four of the senior nuns led by the head abbess carried something wrapped in a white cloth. As they removed the material, it became apparent that it was the corpse of Kama Jhimba, one of the oldest nuns, who had died this morning. The nuns made a sternal to pubic incision along the midline of her body as if they were conducting a public autopsy. Her organs were thrown across the hilltop. Each of her limbs was dismembered. The *anis* descended. Soon after, the vultures arrived. They began to devour Kama Jhimba's remains. I had just witnessed a sky burial.

The *anis* were stoic, but I shook with emotion. Returning one's body to the earth in this way makes perfect sense to me, and yet this sky burial seemed gruesome and cold. It was so final. My grandmother told me that in Iran, before Islam-instituted burials, our dead were also left to face the elements of nature. I would have never been able to do this with Aria's remains. Instead, we hired a stranger to burn her to ashes, which we scattered into cherry blossom trees in Discovery Park and at Lakeview Elementary.

I remember very few details about Aria's memorial service. The most useful thing about it was that it gave me something to do immediately after her death. There were letters to write, a space to find, flowers and food to order, a ceremony to create, and thank-you notes to compose. One day I will watch the videotape you commissioned of the event. Though I was only a ghost participant, I know that the memorial was an important gathering for our community, a safe, time-limited forum to express grief and pay respect.

As I studied these nuns chopping Kama Jhimba's body into pieces and feeding her to the vultures, I knew that I would never understand death. We are forever changed by the death of those we love. Nevertheless, how we mark that passage and move forward may be as different as the sound of Mr. Saito's moving violin concerto, which I remember vividly, to the haunting call of these bone trumpets, which I shall never forget.

Love,
Jasmine

September 12, 1997

Dear Child That Was Never Meant to Be,

On March 5, 1977, I ended my first pregnancy, i.e., terminated my chance of bringing you into this cruel and beautiful world. I walked into the clinic with my best friend, Dottie, who is like the sister I never had. I sat among the women in the waiting room, some accompanied by their boyfriends or husbands, others with their mothers beside them or friends. I filled out my own medical history. I checked off the "yes" box to the "Are you having sex?" question. This sounds easier than it was, even though that was obviously the reason why I was there. Preposterous as it sounds, checking that box was harder for me than signing the consent form, the one that said "I recognize that with any surgical procedure there are risks including cardiac arrest, brain damage, and death."

A girl in my family does not admit to having sex outside of marriage. It is unforgivable, the same as being a whore. "Giving away your treasure chest to any man but your husband would be the worst mistake of your life," my mother always warned me. When I was five years old in swimming class, I remember that my maman would not even let me undress in the girls' locker room. That would mean exposing my "prize," my "sacred curtain," if only to other females.

I did not have you vacuumed from my uterus because of fear or shame of being found out by Maman and Baba. It would have been bad, I mean *really* bad, but I could have dealt with that. I marked "very comfortable" on the form asking how I felt with my decision to terminate the pregnancy because I knew in my heart that now was not the right time, that I would be robbing both of us of a promising future. I was a senior in college with big dreams for my life. I wanted to be a doctor. Even though I have always loved children, I was not ready. I also did not want to bring you up alone.

Your father, Carlos, left us shortly after I told him about you. He disappeared without a word of advice or help. Dottie reminded me of the warning signs, which I admittedly ignored. His father later called to tell me that he was in some monastery in eastern Thailand. He had become a Buddhist monk who swore off all worldly attachments, including money, his hair, you and me. He was in search of Nirvana, that ultimate freedom: "Before studying Buddhism, I thought freedom was about the right to vote or not having to sit at the back of the bus or an inmate who finally leaves prison. But I was wrong. Freedom is about cutting off and eliminating a rigid persistence of basic needs. If you are hungry, you want food; if you are cold, you want clothing; if you are sick, you need your mother's and father's love. As you grow older, these many needs accumulate in the heart and mind to trigger emotions, creating every kind of possible sorrow. Freedom is about letting go of all of these attachments, all of these figments of the mind." In that same monologue, the morning after our condom broke, he said that our happiness, our love for one another, was "fool's gold, a fleeting thought." You and I would have been just one more roadblock in his life.

So it is ironic that twenty years later, I find myself in your father's footsteps in a Buddhist nunnery doing some soul-searching of my own. A horrible accident has detached me from the person I loved most in life, my daughter, Aria. In my weakest moments, I have wondered whether this is my punishment for abandoning you. But mostly, I accept that I did the best that I could for both of us, given the circumstances.

When the long needles pierced my cervix, I did not squirm, even though I was so sad about losing you forever and an industrial-strength cramp ripped through my body. The doctor told me what she was doing at every step. She guided me through the whole thing, even warning me about the noise of the vacuum aspirator machine. Helen Reddy's "I Am Woman" was playing on the radio, and I remember it had not even finished before it was all over. "Jasmine, honey, your abortion is complete. Congratulations. You are no longer pregnant." I was so overwhelmed with relief that I even told a joke once that noisy vacuum had been turned off: "Now I know what it feels like to be a carpet!" Dottie, the medical assistant, and even the doctor burst into laughter as I wiped away my tears.

I told them I wanted to see you before they disposed of you. The doctor warned me it might be traumatic. That I might see identifiable parts and an amorphous tissue called the decidua. I told her I did not care. After all, I had majored in biology and did not get queasy over anatomy. Dot, who is generally more excited by biology than I, could not bear to look. I told the doctor I wanted to see what I had created, wanted to take responsibility for what I had done. The doctor almost gave me a hug right then and there until she realized she still had on her bloody gloves. Then she brought you out in a petri dish.

You were tiny, about the size of a large fingernail, with miniature translucent hands and feet. The doctor pointed out the placenta and your umbilical cord. I cried again, but those were not just tears of sadness, all the what-ifs and wish-it-was-not-sos. They were my first tears of adulthood, recognizing how difficult life can be and yet feeling grateful for the choices I had.

I am so sorry that I had to stop you from growing into existence. I hope you understand. Good-bye, sweet ghost baby who was never meant to be. I hope you left this world knowing that I did the best that I could.

Love,
Jasmine

September 15, 1997

Dear Dottie,

A month has passed since I first entered the BerTse Nunnery, desperate to detach from my world. In meditation, I hoped for a chance to revise and redirect, figure out how to keep walking with these permanent blisters on my feet. After sitting with myself for hours a day, doing nothing more than inhaling and exhaling, I now know that I cannot uncling from my past. In fact, Mamani Joon is my most frequent visitor to the cave.

Maybe this is going to sound overly Shakespearean or Greek tragedy to you, but is it mere coincidence that my grandmother and I both fell in love with men not sanctioned by our parents and who abandoned us by their untimely deaths? How could history repeat itself so closely? Mamani Joon, like I, found some solace in having a child. In flashbacks I return most frequently to those early days of my childhood when she took care of me. I have been replaying my memories of trying to save her and am trying to release the disappointment in failing to do so:

> "Mamani Joon, please stop smoking," I beg. She responds with her characteristic laugh from deep inside the belly that ends in her smoker's wheeze. "Please, Mamani Joon," I plead. "Those cigarettes will kill you. What will I do if you get lung cancer?" My grandmother hugs me close, sees how upset I am. She promises to stop smoking for my sake.

She hands over her cigarettes and I ration them out to her. I hide her Marlboros in all the most difficult places: above our crystal chandelier, behind the toilet bowl scrubber, under the washing machine. I reveal these hiding places to Maman in English while Mamani Joon cooks our dinner. It is when I find Mamani Joon standing on the dining-room table reaching for her cigarettes atop the chandelier that I discover her secret, convenient knowledge of English.

After I catch her in this act, she tries another strategy. She runs to the nearby mini-mart while I am at school and hides the cigarettes in her bosom. Afterward, she chews a mint leaf, hoping I do not catch the smoke on her breath when I give her a kiss. I am not so easily fooled. I imagine her lungs black like the pictures I see on TV. I start to cry. She pulls me close to her large, saggy breasts: "My precious soul, I will outlive everybody. No more worrying about me. Promise?"

When Mamani Joon leaves me to return to her homeland, it hits me that Mamani Joon could die of cancer while in Iran and I will never see her again. "Promise me you will stop smoking?" I plead for the thousandth time. I cry, grab her close, climb onto the familiar space of her lap, and kiss her nose countless times. "I want to save you, Mamani Joon. Let me save you. Please let me save you."

In fact, my grandmother survived two heart attacks and never had cancer. But the congestive heart failure finally caught up with her. In her dying days, our relatives were at her disposal, entertaining her with jokes and stories, doing the grocery shopping and cooking for her, staying with her during the night when she could no longer breathe. Maman told me that my grandmother's morale blossomed when she returned home, and it never deteriorated again despite a failing body.

I am sure there is a message for me here, only I am unable to decipher it. Perhaps my grandmother is pulling me toward Iran, finally making me fulfill my promise of visiting her home country. In Tibet I have realized that I want to better understand the history of my family. This much I know from Mamani Joon: Besides the occasional pilgrimage to Mecca and the nomadic wanderings through the Persian empire, no grand journeys have split apart the family until my parents' voyage. Nothing has been lost in migration or translation. We can trace our ancestors back for centuries to Shah 'Abbas during the days of the Islamic Renaissance, when the capital city of Esfahan must have truly felt like *nesfeh jahan* (half the world). The land has not changed hands much over the generations, roughly speaking, nor has the connectedness of the people.

Here I am, a well-educated adult whose professional life involves eliciting life stories from my patients, and yet I know so little about the lives of my parents and relatives. Why had it not occurred to me to ask these questions? How much of my life did Aria understand? Would she know me if we met in an afterlife? What would I have told her?

Deprived of the motherhood that I assumed would accompany me to my death, I find myself a stranger in this cave. I must rebuild my self, starting from my deepest foundations, my ignored heritage.

Love,
Jasmine

September 18, 1997

Dear Maman,

Once, when four-month-old Aria was in my arms, I slipped on my way down the stairs. You have not seen my house in Seattle, where I moved to be near Dottie once Justin died, but I can assure you that the stairs are steep with hardwood floors. Aria flew into the air, and miraculously I managed to catch her upright while we slid down those stairs together, gashing my knees all the way down. Aria did not seem traumatized at all. In fact, she laughed as though she had been tossed like pizza dough, and not even one bruise marked her tiny body.

I do not know what I would have done to myself if I had hurt her. For all intents and purposes, at that point she was no more than a sleeping, eating, and excreting creature totally dependent upon my attention. Yet the bond I had with her even in those early infant days was unlike anything I had ever experienced. She was a piece of Justin, our epilogue. But, Maman, Aria was also the future for you and Baba.

There were many moments like those when I had a palpable taste of the maternal connection, when I realized how much you and Baba must love me. How is it that we have not spoken in over seven years nor embraced for a decade? You never understood me, but that is not the point. My pride and stubbornness have taken me away from you, and now I can imagine how horrible you must feel.

Our estrangement is reversible. I will finally come visit you in Iran. I am so sorry.

Love,
Your Yasaman

September 26, 1997

Dear Dottie,

My time in the *ani gompa* has come to a close. I have grown fond of these nuns. I laugh hysterically at their juvenile jokes, like when they come up behind me and grab my hair, threatening to cut it off with the shears for the juniper bushes. Our communication will never be complex, but somehow we are able to say enough. This morning, as I awaited my pickup by Land Rover, Kama Shoompy and Kama Yondrew were feverishly paging through my phrase book. They showed their findings to Kama Bamoo, who has the nicest script, and wrote me a final message as I hugged them good-bye. "We You Love," Kama Bamoo copied in perfect English letters. I teared up.

I am being called back to where I came from: the old country. I have given up too quickly on my parents, who gave me everything except the permission to live in the modern American world in which they conceived and raised me. Mamani Joon, Justin, and Aria are gone, but there is hope for me to reconnect with my parents.

I will go to Iran, to find what is left of my family. I have almost allowed my roots to be dropped into the Atlantic Ocean like fish eggs that separate from an osprey's talons in midflight, but I think I can reclaim them. I have let my relationship with Maman and Baba be severed for the last several years, but I will beg them for forgiveness. A fierce wind sends my message of remorse across the Himalayas to the foothills of the Elburz Mountains. I follow.

Love,
Jasmine

TELEGRAM

To: Maryam and Hasan Talahi

From: Yasaman Talahi

Date: September 30, 1997

Maman & Baba Joon: I am now in Tibet, coming home to Iran. Miss you so much. Arrival: October 2, 2:30 A.M., Air France #673. Please be there. Love you. *Ghorbaneh shoma.*

September 6, 1997

My dear meditator,

I don't know how you do it. Today I tried meditation just to get a sense of what you're going through out there in Tibet. I downloaded "Meditation for Beginners" from the Bodhi Web site. Of course with my knee problems, I didn't even attempt lotus position. So I just sat on my bed, legs sprawled in no particular direction, and focused on the path of my breathing like they said to do in the guide. Before I'd followed my breath down my lungs to my internal organs and little toes, yours truly was on snooze patrol. I thought about repeating the exercise in a meat locker to truly be at one with your experience. Do you stay awake by shivering?

I miss Aria so much I actually feel physical pain over it. I can't imagine how you make it through each day trekking in foreign lands. When I start to feel bad, the last thing I want to do is leave my home. I put on my sweatpants, heat up some Swiss Miss, and make an art out of moping. But then again, before your decision to leave Seattle, you were never one to sit still with your emotions. I can't imagine what your meditation retreat will be like. That much quiet and alone time would surely make me crazy (nuttier than baseline, that is!). Nevertheless, thank the goddess, you've escaped the suicidal bike warriors of Chengdu. I, for one, am never going to China. What with all the staring they do, can you imagine how many accidents I'd cause per day? Speaking of bicycles, did I tell you that I ordered a little person's mountain bike from the LPA home page? It was a great discovery. You should see how fast I zoom to the university on the Burke-Gilman Trail.

I admire your patience for lengthy correspondence. Sometimes I get so wrapped up in your travelogue that I forget to be mad at you. What's really going on with you, Jazz? How can you stand to be so far away from me? I hope that quiet time in a cave will make you see that you can't fully recover by escaping. How much longer do you plan to wander the world until you realize that true healing won't happen until you make your peace with Seattle? Don't you think it's only here where you can truly face the loss of your daughter in the company of the two of us who are so entwined with your life and hers? I promise not to stop my campaign until Operation Return Jasmine Home is successful!

Reading your fascinating, vivid letters makes me feel guilty for how little progress I've made on my dissertation. Here you are in the middle of mourning, not to mention negotiating the challenges of third-world travel, and you are able to churn out tomes of insightful material. Before February 17, I was already procrastinator extraordinaire when it came to my dissertation. But now? Every time I sit down to write, memories of Aria cycle through my brain and I pretty much end up bawling. The only thing to do in response is to get out of my office and be nice to myself.

One of the best things I've started since you left is a mentorship program for dwarf teens in the greater Seattle area, especially the ones with AP parents. Three of them (two achondroplast girls and one boy with diastrophic dysplasia) come regularly to our bimonthly get-togethers, and sometimes even a fourth achon girl shows up. You know, I was always so disappointed that Teddy and Belle didn't have another kid. I asked my mama about it once. She got squirmy polite on me, to the point where I knew she was flat-out lying, but I didn't press her on it. "You were all I ever wanted, sweetheart." Between all the medical problems and constant staring, it takes extra effort for parents of dwarfs to do the job right. I want to help with that. I want to make the dwarf teens feel like what they're going through is normal. Plus, we just plain have a lot of fun. You should see us at the movies. We definitely draw more attention than the previews.

Those kids help fill the void left by Aria in my life. I instantly fell in love with the little munchkin as if she were my very own, but what I didn't understand was how much you and she provided a family for me. I always imagined getting married and having kids of my own, but there haven't exactly been too many dashing father figures throwing themselves at my feet. Thank the goddess, I'm at peace with not doing it on my own, especially after seeing you go through it. Having these youngsters in my life, like spending time with Aria, keeps me grounded (not that I am too far from the ground to start with!) and gives me perspective on what's important in life.

Speaking of which, get your little self back here ASAP!

Love,
Dot

August 9, 1997

Jasmine,

You're making me crazy. I can forgive you for having left the country. In the past it's been my instinct too. But I'm angry to be left behind, to not be able to communicate with you. You've shut me out. You've made me the saddest and loneliest guy in the universe. Worst of all, I've let you do this. For Christ's sake, Jasmine, I loved Aria too. It's true, I never had a burning desire to be a father, but my heart was open to the possibility. I fell in love with you as a mother, and Aria was very much a part of that package. I wasn't used to taking care of small children in the beginning, but I know you saw the strong relationship that eventually developed between Aria and me. I don't know how you can simply dismiss my role in raising Aria or step away from our relationship.

You know I've had issues with getting mad at the intimate people in my life. Both Dot and my therapist have helped me realize how unhealthy it is to not get mad. I've come to the conclusion that my repressed anger is the biggest scar of my childhood. Sometimes I feel like I get it, and other times I've actually punched a hole in my wall in frustration. I don't understand why you constantly imagine yourself not coming back to me. Your words can be so loving and at once so cold. I don't know how you could've stopped writing to me, how you seem to have given up on us for good. It's crazy to think that you can somehow release me into the world as if I'm capable of "proceeding" with my life and simply erasing memories of you and Aria.

I feel so stupid for not making this all clear before you left, and god knows Dot's made no secret of blaming me. Tomorrow I'm going to Platte, where at least I know my efforts will be appreciated. Ma slipped in the kitchen yesterday and broke her hip. She's still in the hospital after an emergency operation. Her doctor says she'll be okay. I'm not too worried—she's the heartiest one of the Forsythe bunch. Dad's the one who seems to need my help the most. He's all broken up over this.

I pray that long meditations in the Himalayas will make you see the truth—that I love you despite the hell you've put me through and that our relationship is worth rebuilding. What happened to Aria is the worst event of my life. Losing you on top of that feels unbearable.

Write to me, Jasmine. Better yet, please come home.

Alexander

CHAPTER V

Islamic Republic of Iran Post Corporation
International Facsimile Service

In the name of God, the benevolent, the merciful.

To: Dorothy Wilkins & Alexander Forsythe
University of Washington, Anthropology Dept.
Fax Number: 01-206-543-3285
From: Jasmine Talahi
Date: October 10, 1997

My dears,

I marinated in self-doubt. I waited until the final boarding call. Did I have the courage to face a decade's worth of family banishment? Would my parents accept my apologies or skewer me further for my American sins? Would we continue to feel estranged from one another? And what about traveling to the birthplace of Islamic fundamentalism on an American passport, where Americans were taken hostage for 444 days? These questions churned my stomach and gave me pause. I squeezed the black head scarf in my handbag as if it were some kind of security blanket and took a deep breath. I walked to the gate and boarded the plane.

Upon entering the aircraft, I was taken aback by the many pairs of eyes focused on me: dark, curious, inviting. These were bold gazes that did not turn away in discomfort. I had already been transported to a different world. The flight attendants seemed impatient with us. As reunions took place along the aisles and conversations extended across rows, the purser announced for a second time in French and then in English that everyone should take their seats and fasten their seat belts.

Brooding, melancholic music played overhead. It was unfamiliar, stringed of some sort, and difficult to hear between the excited hum of conversations between strangers. It was odd to be in a place where everyone looked like they could be related to me. A woman living in Paris, all Givenchy and Louis Vuitton, was going home for the first time in eighteen years to bring back carpets for her import-export business. A man based in Stockholm planned to visit his ailing mother. A pair of sisters from Los Angeles, six and eight, were fighting over who would get the first chance to hold their baby cousin yet unseen. It struck me minutes later that no English had been spoken. My grandmother's tongue, neglected for almost thirty-five years, was forgetting that it was forgotten.

Hours passed like minutes. The next thing I knew the flight attendants were erasing all evidence of the in-flight cocktails and a wardrobe transformation was beginning. I took out my veil from my carry-on bag, required public uniform for any female older than nine in the Islamic Republic. The veil was a kind of portable wall for women, keeping non-intimate male eyes away from the supposed secret paradise behind it. The Iranian dress code mandates head-to-toe covering, although the face and hands can be exposed. In Chengdu, on my return trip from Lhasa, I found an ankle-length dusty olive overcoat manteau and plain black scarf *roosari* to cover my hair. I put on my costume while Coco Chanel on my left wiped away her lipstick. In a few seconds she became a respectable Islamic sister, vices hidden by an all-enveloping, half-moon-shaped black chador. I wondered why she put on the makeup in the first place.

In the West we veil nuns and brides. Once, when I was Aria's age, I pulled down the *roosari* of an elderly Iranian woman, a friend of my grandmother's. I wanted to see if she had any hair beneath the fabric. Mamani Joon scolded me harshly, an unusual occurrence. She told me that peeking behind a veil would bring me a glimpse of death. I never did it again.

At the modern Mehrabad Airport, I was first greeted by the holy dyad, huge color photographs of bearded men: the current supreme religious leader Ali Khamenei beside the imam, Ayatollah Ruhollah Khomeini, images that I have seen over and over again. I wondered why the recently elected President Khatami was not represented. I had no problems at passport check. A young woman in a black chador with gold-rimmed glasses hiding honey-colored eyes said to me in Persian, "Born in America to Iranian parents. First trip to Iran. Okay.

Welcome home!" It was four in the morning Tehran time when I emerged from customs to the arrival hall. Restless children waiting for hours pushed for the best view through the glass. Most noticeable were the women in black chadors who seemed to blend together like a flock of crows.

I saw two middle-aged men who must have been brothers run toward each other and lock in an embrace. My heart ached. I searched for my elderly parents. Their last visit to the States was in 1987, just before I met Justin. They had stopped urging me to come visit them in Iran during the war with Iraq, and after the summer of 1990 they had ceased contact with me altogether. On this first trip to Iran, I was not sure how I should feel. I did not even know what my relatives looked like, nor did I know most of their names. Nevertheless, I found myself waving enthusiastically through the window. The eyes on the other side of that glass were so expectant. Was I greeting family I did not yet know?

They grabbed me all at once. My mother seemed shorter than I remembered. My father could only hobble now. I was so overwhelmed by the faces that I tried to calm myself by counting the relatives that had come to pick me up (forty-seven). My cheeks ached from multiple kisses from family I never knew existed. I did not notice the tears spilling from my cheeks until a young cousin pointed at me and announced loudly to the group: "Look, Aunt Yasaman is crying." The children, hyperactive from the anticipation and the late hour, argued with each other over who would sit beside me on the car ride home. I tried to speak Persian, but the words felt clumsy, as if my mouth were recovering from dental surgery.

My relatives piled into their seven collective cars, and we zoomed through the wide streets of Tehran, past the illuminated white Y-shaped arch of the Freedom Monument, to my parents' home near Revolution Square. Even at 5 A.M., you could smell the grilled meat at the kebab restaurant on the first floor of their concrete building. My parents live in a two-bedroom apartment with a huge living-room area for entertaining guests and both a Western and Iranian toilet (for those who prefer to squat). I recognized the silky Persian carpets that covered the floors of each room and gave character to a place with surprisingly few decorations and sparse furnishings. There is a horseshoe-shaped blue velvet couch and an out-of-place crystal chandelier in the living room, a modern wide-screen television set, and a large golden samovar that still works. There is also a dining-room table with ten chairs, but mostly people sit on the colorful brocaded cushions on the floor. There is a huge painting of me on my tenth birthday in a gold-painted wooden frame, and a black-and-white wedding photo of my parents, but very little material evidence of their Western life.

I expected we would all go to bed upon arriving, but instead my relatives crowded into my parents' home. A beautiful embroidered tablecloth with Persian calligraphy was spread on the floor, and we feasted on a typical Iranian breakfast of flat bread and feta cheese, cucumbers, herbs, walnuts, quince jam, fruit, and tea.

Everyone seemed to know about Aria, and yet no one mentioned her out-of-wedlock conception. I noticed that the adults were mostly wearing black. My aunt Fereshteh, Maman's youngest sister, made sure I understood that it was on Aria's behalf. The relatives kept repeating *"Chesme-tun row-shan!"* ("How bright your eyes are!") to my parents, a congratulations for my long-overdue arrival, despite its sad context. Young cousins anxious to predict good fortunes for me leafed through the poetry books of Hafez. After the solitude of Tibet and the long flight from China, I was drunk from all this attention. Two of Maman's sisters took a break to do their morning prayer, but no one else joined them. By 9 A.M. everyone had left, and my parents and I finally went to bed.

We have had several days of these types of visits, and they all blur together now. I have hardly seen Tehran beyond the dense smog, the choked streets, the architecturally bland high-rises, the numerous construction sites, the clumps of similarly themed small shops, and the occasional fountain or sculpture in the middle of a plaza or roundabout. The northern part of the city reportedly has mountain views and tree-lined streets, more manicured parks, and villas, but I have not yet been there. There are nice museums in this otherwise uninspiring capital city, but my days are mostly spent in the interior of homes. Since visitors usually come to the elderly, we have been inundated with guests. Sometimes only four to five people come see us, and at other times up to twenty have paid us a visit. People are always filtering in and out, bringing me gifts of flowers; cream-filled, rosewater-scented flaky pastries; Iranian handicrafts; and even gold jewelry. Several family members live in walking distance of my parents' apartment and drop by spontaneously. My mother keeps her silver filigree platters heaped with fruit that my father buys from a nearby stand, and the samovar is always on. My consumption is monitored closely and taken as a reflection of my satisfaction with Iran. I have never drunk so much tea.

Thus far, my parents have been on their best behavior. They seem to have forgotten my multiple transgressions. They do not mention Justin nor ask me invasive questions. They send you their warmest regards, Dottie, but mostly they are hungry to hear about Aria. When I tell them stories, their eyes are frequently full of tears. Indeed, conveying condolence seems to be a forte of Iranian culture. Being in Iran, where every relative shares in my losses though none has ever met Aria, has brought my self-centered grieving into clear focus. How could I have turned my back on the two of you? Why have I not acknowledged your sadness? Both of you have played an integral role in raising my daughter, and yet I have been myopic beyond my own pain. I am ashamed of my behavior, and yet none of this mitigates my need to be here.

With deepest apologies to you both and much love,
Jasmine

October 26, 1997

Dear Dot,

Maman and I have forged a kind of unspoken truce. At first I did not trust our easygoing reconnection. I was convinced the superficial peace would eventually revert to our antagonistic dynamics from my adolescence. Time has changed us. No more niggling questions from her that automatically imply my guilt or failure like: Do you care about your family and heritage? When will you ever think about someone other than yourself? Why not make yourself more marriageable? How about opening up a private practice so you can make really good money? In fact, Maman hardly asks me questions at all. I keep waiting for the "Do you have a special person in your life?" line of inquiry, but thus far I have been safe from any kind of prying. Maman has even been careful talking about Aria, allowing me to unfold at my own pace. Though I do not yet fully trust the new level of acceptance in our relationship, I am hopeful that it will continue. It is easier not to talk about the fractious past, as much as I want to apologize for my role in keeping us apart. Maman has chatted with me about our relatives, her childhood, my father's health, and all the other stories she has meant to tell me in the decade since we have had a real conversation. We are not often alone, as friends and relatives constantly drop by. But this morning she began talking about her relationship with me and Mamani Joon.

"Yasaman Joon, do you know what a stubborn child you were?" We were sitting on the floor of the living room, our backs against the couch, sorting out the dirt and stones in a large platter of rice in front of us. I shook my head, as I had envisioned myself a terribly obedient and polite daughter.

"You would decide something and that was it. There was no changing your mind. After you turned two, you decided you were too big for diapers. In fact, you thought of yourself as a tiny adult and could not stand it when people referred to you as a baby. In the meanwhile, you still did not have good control over your bladder and would wet your pants once or twice a day and usually at night. I was tired of changing your clothes during the day, but no amount of lobbying on my part could convince you to wear a diaper, not even for backup. If I forced you to put one on, I would soon see your pants on the floor and your diaper proudly hanging in your hand. Your father saw my frustration one evening and even spanked you over your refusal, but that did not help either.

"You would only listen to your grandmother. She had a way with you that no one else did. She told me to buy incontinence pads for the elderly and then showed you how she put one on herself. After that you agreed to use a diaper at night.

"I wanted you to stay my baby. You were growing up too fast, and I was not home to witness it. My retarded kids at the group home needed me so much more than you, and I used to resent that. I was thirty-seven years old when I was pregnant with you, and I used to worry that you would turn out to have mongolism or some other deformity. Later on a part of me always thought it would have been easier on me to have a dependent child. That way you would always be attached to me, and we would not be separated even in your adulthood. Unlucky for me, dependence was never a part of your nature, not even from the beginning.

"Your grandmother was a tremendous help to us. It was because of her that we survived financially in America. But I was angry that I was forced to work and silently cursed your father for not being able to provide for us in this new country. Before the Revolution, I was a spoiled bourgeoisie who had grown up with maids and drivers. I hardly had to lift a finger. Once I married, I grew so bored and frustrated trying to have a child, that I perfected my study of foreign languages. First French, then English. I gave lessons to wealthy children in the neighborhood. I even joined a volleyball team. The truth is, before trying to get pregnant, I had never failed at anything. Of course, I have been humbled in a million ways since then." She looked right through me then, and I imagined Maman would begin to list the multitude of ways in which I had caused her pain, but she said nothing more.

Much of my time in Iran has been spent this way, talking with my mother and other female relatives as we work through the domestic chores of the day. Maman tells me I am emulating my grandmother's era when women spent most of their time with their children indoors in the quarters (called the *andarooni*) formally separated from the men. Baba is surprisingly mobile for his age, despite the use of a cane from osteoarthritis of the hip and the damaged pavement of Tehran sidewalks, lining canals of open sewage. He is often out visiting friends, buying household items, and to this day still negotiating deals in the bazaar, coming home by 2 P.M. for the afternoon meal. On the other hand, I have lost patience for the outside world. Inside the privacy of my parents' home, I do not have to face the fashion police, those watchdogs of social behavior who enforce the public dress code; the suffocating pollution; aggressive drivers with their constant honking; and bored groups of men who are eager to harass a lone woman as she passes.

After all this time, I have only now realized my mother's amazing talent for storytelling. Her seventy-nine-year-old memory seems to retain every detail from the past, even ones that have been handed down from generations gone by. In the United States, there are so many forms of entertainment that we have lost the art of oral history. Even though my mother was a gifted entertainer, there was no forum for her to express herself in the States. In Iran the limited state-controlled television, ban on VCRs, and restricted options for nightlife conspire to make in-house activities the major form of diversion. I watch my mother weave complex narratives that endlessly amuse our family and friends and realize that I am just beginning to know her.

We often sit on the carpet and tend to the daily food issues. Cleaning and sorting through the fresh herbs we will use in that day's cooking, Maman points out the different varieties and names them for me in Persian: basil, cilantro, marjoram, parsley, dill, lovage, and mint. The downstairs neighbors and Aunt Fereshteh have left after a cup of midmorning tea. More guests are expected for lunch. As we sit in huge piles of greens, she tells me the story of Mamani Joon's lifelong smoking career.

It turns out that my mother and my grandmother were close allies, despite their predictable quarrels. Though Maman abhorred smoke, she admired Mamani Joon's brazen habit, which was quite unusual for women of her time. Apparently, Mamani Joon started smoking at the age of ten. Her father, Agha Baba, was a trader who had brought back a chest full of Golfalak cigarettes from the Gulf of Oman. They were kept in the underground storage of the house, where an unusually fierce rainstorm had ruined them. Or so her father had assumed. Mamani Joon dared her three friends to weave through the sacks of wheat, barley, and wool in the dark basement where snakes and scorpions were known to congregate. When they reached the chest, my grandmother started digging for dry cigarette packs.

It was true that the cigarettes on top were very soggy, but at the very bottom, she found what she was seeking. The girls stole matches from the kitchen, and my grandmother was the first one to light up. She took a puff, trying to mimic her father's deep inhalation, but instead started coughing and felt the world spin around her. Her friends laughed as they watched her, themselves hesitant to inhale.

Eventually, the foursome formed their own little smoking club in the underground, with Mamani Joon as their ringleader. Augmenting their forbidden behaviors, they started reading poetry in that secret space. Afterward, the girls ran around outdoors, hoping to air out their clothes, and chewed on mint leaves to hide their smoky breath. It appears that Mamani Joon's attempts to cover up her tobacco habit have been long-standing.

Love,
Jasmine

November 6, 1997

Dear Dottie,

Some days I think I am regaining normalcy. Then I have a sudden setback that makes me realize how far I have to go. Today was one of those days. The incident started without any warning. I had run out of toothpaste, and I asked Maman if she had any that I could borrow. She directed me to her medicine cabinet, which I opened without second thought. There, on the top shelf, I came upon a yellow bottle of Johnson's Baby Shampoo. I held the half-empty bottle close to my heart. I opened the bottle and inhaled deeply, remembering the last time I had used it to wash Aria's thick hair. I remembered her strange bath phobia: how she would cry as soon as she heard the water running, but once she was all wet, she had such a good time that I actually had to pry her out. On the way out of the last bath of her life, she stepped on her rubber ducky and it squeaked loudly in protest. Aria picked it up, kissed it several times on its head, and apologized profusely for hurting it. As I recalled this image of my daughter, I burst into tears and could not gain control over myself.

Maman wandered into the bathroom wondering if I had found the toothpaste. She saw me kneeling on the ground, my head leaning on the sink. I choked on my words as I tried to explain and instead pointed to the shampoo bottle. Whether she understood me or not, Maman sat with me for several minutes and then let me be. When I finally left the bathroom, she brought me some tea with a little container full of sugar lumps (not even my mother could believe that I drink my tea black), and the two of us leaned against the velvet couch in silence, listening to the purr of boiling tea in the samovar.

Once I had regained my composure, I could not bear to talk about the incident. I told her a similar anecdote about the days following Aria's death. She closed her eyes because I do not think she could bear to look at me. Did I ever tell you this story?

In the early days after the accident, while looking through Aria's backpack, I found a half-eaten Tootsie Roll. I had no idea who had given this to Aria—as you know, I did not allow candy into our household. My mother smiled in recognition. I put the hardened, sticky roll with its accompanying wrapper into my mouth. I left it there, barely chewing, until it dissolved completely. I was reluctant to swallow it. Another good-bye. That waxy paper with its last bits of sweetness was all I had left of Aria. That and her last pair of shoes, those beat-up pink Keds that she loved so much. I had not allowed her to wear them to school. What if I had thrown them away? Would she have run any slower or faster in other shoes? Could she have dodged Stephanie's car then? And since when did Aria like Tootsie Rolls? Was I wrong to ban candy in our house? Who had given her the candy anyway? Would she have tried to keep it a secret from me? Am I a bad mother for not knowing these things?

Maman put both of her hands on mine, as if to shush me in the most loving way possible, and said: "You understand now, Yasaman Joon. Being a mother is the hardest responsibility we face in this life."

Despite this new bonding, there are times when I have desperately wanted to be alone, back in my cave for just a few moments. Solitude has always been a comforting place for me, clearly an American trait. Unfortunately, introversion is not a concept well understood in my family. My relatives are anxious to exhibit their love for me at all times. This involves constant company, even when they do not know what to say. After lunch I often go through the motions of joining my family in a siesta. We have rolled-up mattresses with sheets, blankets, and pillows to accommodate up to a dozen guests. I retire to my room, climb under the blanket, and am ready to feign sleep should they peek in on me. Some of my most cherished moments have been during this postprandial calm, when I have written you letters to the snores of my father next door, the smells lingering from the *chelow-kabob* restaurant below, and the outside bustle of the streets finally comes to a temporary halt.

Love,
Jasmine

November 14, 1997

Aria Joon,

You would love Iran: all the family, so much attention. You would never feel like an only child in Iran. Mama cannot even count how many cousins we have here. What is a cousin anyway? In the States we rarely consider fourth- and fifth-degree relatives as family, but in Iran they stop by our house at all times. They are all a part of us.

You know what? Everyone loves you here. You are so alive in our thoughts and stories.

I visited Mamani Joon's grave today. After all these years, I finally said good-bye to my grandmother. But I could not bear to part with you. Not yet.

I miss you so much. Maybe I am waiting to say good-bye so that I can hug you one more time, if only in sleep.

As funny as this will sound, I forgive you for dying. And I am so grateful that you brought me here.

Mama loves you forever and ever.

December 2, 1997

Dear Dot,

I am obsessed with Mamani Joon stories. My mother delights in telling me tales from the past, and there is no end to my interest. I keep wondering if we will ever have a painful, cathartic conversation about our relationship or whether we will continue with this new normal of sticking to safe topics.

Maman has become tiny in her old age, with the hump back of osteoporosis, sunken cheeks, and long silver hair that she wears in a single, elegant braid down her back. She is in good health, despite arthritis, controlled high blood pressure, and bothersome varicose veins. Her voice is high-pitched and singsongy, which makes her sound more fragile than she is. Her hands are generally always busy, whether she is cooking, cleaning, or fixing a broken appliance. After she awakens from her afternoon nap, she leaves her bed to lie on the couch and wait for the others to awaken. Leaning on one elbow, she supports her head, as if she were in classical opium-smoking position, and turns on the television. If I join her, she turns off the program and asks if I want to hear another story. Were I to repeat all that I have heard, it would take longer than reciting the entire *Shahnameh,* the epic book of kings. My relatives find my curiosity in our shared history charming, and now feed me stories along with large platters of rice and fragrant stews.

Today I learned that during all these months of story-telling, Maman has shielded me from the most painful and yet most fundamental part of Mamani Joon's past. It suddenly occurred to me that after months of hearing Mamani Joon stories, I never knew whether she regretted having only sons. My mother looked at me from the couch and paused. "Do you really want to know the truth?" she asked. I nodded without ambivalence.

It turns out that my grandmother wanted daughters from the very beginning. She was not at all concerned about having sons in a time when sons were all that mattered. After she gave birth to my father, she was determined to have a girl. Three months after Hasan was born, she was pregnant again. She was sure it was a girl this time. The midwife had said so when she had examined the color of Mamani Joon's nipples. The fortune-teller confirmed it upon looking at the pattern of dregs of Turkish coffee left in her cup. She had dreams about it and she was right.

Tuba was a fat, ruddy girl who came into this world not a day early and not a day late. Mamani Joon was so happy. Unfortunately, Tuba was taken away from her the day after she was born. Her husband and mother were concerned that Hasan, who was nearly one by this time, would be deprived of breast milk if she also fed Tuba. So they forced my grandmother to relinquish Tuba to a wet nurse.

Goli was the best wet nurse in town. The poor woman had been pregnant nine times in as many years, but all of those pregnancies resulted in late miscarriages. The wet nurse had extra milk and no children of her own to feed, so she marketed her precious commodity to women like my grandmother, who had back-to-back pregnancies and were in need of milk. Mamani Joon did not want to give up this child of hers to the wet nurse, no matter how excellent she was rumored to be. In those days the infant would live with the wet nurse along with two or three other infants, and the mothers would come by for daily visits. My grandmother did not win this battle. Every one of our relatives believed it was the logical choice and the right decision.

Tuba seemed to be doing well despite the deprivation from her mother. This wet nurse was only feeding one other child at the time and had taken a strong liking to the baby girl. In the meanwhile, my grandmother decided that once Hasan received twenty months of breast milk, it was time to take Tuba back, even though two to three full years was the standard length of breast-feeding. Two weeks before she was to be brought back to her own house, Tuba developed a high fever. When she had a seizure, the wet nurse brought her to my grandmother's house. By then it was too late. Tuba died the next day.

Mamani Joon plunged deeply into grief again. Back then, infant mortality was commonplace, a fact of life, and yet Mamani Joon could not accept what had happened to her daughter. She was so depressed that she stopped breast-feeding my father altogether. She refused to have anything to do with her husband or mother. If not for her young son, she may have never recovered. In the end, she could not bear to punish little Hasan for Tuba's death. The poor infant was not responsible for sending Tuba away.

Mamani Joon tried three more times to have a daughter, but with the birth of each subsequent son, she was gravely disappointed. Finally, after the fourth child, she refused to become pregnant again. She douched with lemon and vinegar and took the herbs the midwife prescribed to her to induce infertility. She was successful, for she never became pregnant again, but she also never had another daughter.

I was numb listening to Maman, but when she finished, I knew I needed a release. At four in the afternoon, I put on my overcoat, tied my head scarf extra tight around my neck, and laced up my tennis shoes. I found my dark sunglasses in my coat pocket and put them on. I kissed Maman on both cheeks, making an excuse that I wanted to go out to buy bread for the evening meal. Before she could advise me on which bakery I should visit and exactly how much I should pay, I slammed the door behind me. I started running.

"Laboo, laboo, laboo darim." The peddler advertised his boiled beets ready for eating, the Tehran equivalent of pretzels on a New York corner.

"Namaki, namaki," droned the salt man.

"Tajrish, Tajrish." A taxi driver needed one more passenger to squeeze into his car for the northern part of the city. The car was already full, two men practically on each other's laps in the front seat, and two women in the back. I could smell chicken grilling and ripe fruit at the juice stand. I needed to get away from the people, the noise, and the chaos. Meanwhile, sharp pains accumulated beneath my sternum.

My mobility was limited beneath my heavy coat and scarf, but I ran as fast as I could. My feet pounded the cracked sidewalk as I dodged people who stared at me with curiosity. A group of four men, each with mustaches and three-day shadows, strolled down the street, arms and shoulders interlocked, looking like they had nothing better to do but to cause trouble. One of them had the audacity and the misfortune to try to block my way.

"Let me see those hidden eyes behind your glasses, pretty lady," he teased.

"Go to hell," I shot back with my new words in Persian, not missing a stride. He rubbed his shoulders in pain as I ran through them.

I passed a string of gold shops, one after the other. Another man asked if he could be of any help to me. I shook my head impatiently, *"Nah merci."* No thanks. I longed for the indifference of urban American pedestrians. I ran through a soccer game played by boys in an alley. The plastic ball came in my direction, and I kicked it hard into the goal between two garbage cans. The children cheered, but I did not even crack a smile. I jumped across the open gutter, wondering how my old father or any stiff, fragile person did this on a daily basis. I reached my favorite bakery, where the Turkish men spoke with funnier accents than mine. They waved and invited me in as I whizzed by.

How could this be? My own grandmother suffered through all of this too. She lost her first love and her only daughter. How could I have not known? Why had I not heard of Tuba? Why did my mother and father never tell me about my dead would-have-been aunt? Why had my grandmother's pain been so unspoken in a land where emotions are readily expressed? How could history repeat itself so closely?

I reached the theater in the round. A lone man at least two decades younger than me, who was reading the program for the upcoming week, yelled after me: "My dear queen, my heart stops for you. Why not stop for me?"

"Shut up," I countered. I vowed to myself that no matter how many years passed, every person who was important to me would know about my Aria, and that I would share my family stories with all the important people in my life.

"Copon, copon." A young boy on Vali-Asr Street tried to sell me coupons for subsidized foodstuffs. I ignored him and continued running.

Finally the tears came. Moving through my nose, they ended up as black mucus from all the pollution in the air. I cried for Mamani Joon, and for myself too. It felt good to be alone.

There was only one thing that could have stopped me. I heard the siren, saw the white jeep drive past me, and looked down at the combat boots and machine guns. The morality squad approached me from behind: "Lady, please stop running and approach the vehicle," came the menacing voice through the megaphone from one of the young bearded men. These urban soldiers could have driven up beside me and talked to me in civilized voices, but instead they seemed to be in the mood to intimidate. They parked the car on the corner ahead of me as they waited for my approach. The heat radiated through my cheeks and I tried not to pant. I calmly walked over to their car and did a mental check to make sure I was fully compliant with the Islamic dress code: no makeup, no hair showing, and ankles covered with dark socks.

"Yes?" I inquired, acting as innocent and polite as possible despite my brewing fury. It was not wise to argue with them. From what I had heard, they responded well to demure women and gave the confident, argumentative ones a harder time.

"Dear sister, pray tell: Why are you running?" The officer could not have been more than twenty-one. He had a large acne cyst on his nose and tilted his head back as if to say, "Ah yes, we are going to have fun with this one."

"Excuse me, I was just trying to get some exercise," I responded quietly, eyes turned downward, trying my best to look meek.

"Aha. She is one of those," the driver said to pimple nose. "A jokester. Next she is going to tell us she runs track and field in the Olympics. Sister, do I have to tell you we mean serious business here? Just tell us: Who are you running from?"

"Pardon me?" I was confused.

"Where is your husband?"

"I am not married." My tone was angrier now.

"A pretty woman like you not married?" The men did not believe my story. "Oh, so you were running from your boyfriend's house. Did he reject you today? Is that why you are crying, you poor slut?"

"Excuse me? No, no, no. You do not understand me. Running has nothing to do with my boyfriend. Besides, he lives in the United States."

"Of course he does," said the one in the front seat, elbowing the driver in the ribs with a knowing wink. "Right. That is why you look so American there with those fancy glasses. Surely, they must be a gift from him."

"Actually, I bought them for myself." I could not control my condescension, guns or no guns.

"Sure you did. By the way, we like your fake, heavy American accent. We have not heard one this good in a long time. Have you been watching some contraband American films?"

"This is absolutely ridiculous. I was born and raised in America. Why not go and reprimand someone who is actually breaking the law."

"Sorry, sister, but we are taking you to the *komiteh* station for some further questioning."

"Wait a minute. I did not do anything wrong. What is going on here?"

"If you would just cooperate with us and tell us why you were running, we would let you go. But you must tell us the truth."

They probably would have settled for money, but I could not bring myself to bribe them. How stupid to be arrested for this. "Listen, sirs." I took off my sunglasses and looked at both of them directly in the eyes. "This is my first time in Iran. I have just come from America to visit my family. I was going for a little jog to try to lose some weight after eating all of the delicious food they have been giving me. I am not coming with you in the car." I fumbled for my wallet, thankful for its presence in my coat pocket, and pulled out the evidence. "Look, see. Here is some proof." I showed them my American driver's license.

I handed it to the one in the driver's seat, not thinking about my uncovered head and bare shoulders in the photo. He looked at it, and then he immediately looked away. He was embarrassed, as if now he had really violated me.

"She is not lying," he said to pimple face, handing my license back.

"We are very sorry." This time it actually sounded like he meant it. "Welcome to the Islamic Republic," said the other. Now they were friendly. "Where do you live? Tehrangeles?" referring to the Iranian expatriate mecca of Los Angeles. I shook my head. "New York? Hollywood? Las Vegas?"

"In a state that is north of California." This was not the first time I described it this way for Iranians.

"We apologize again for taking your time, sister. May God watch over you."

"Good-bye," I said, and slowly I walked toward my parents' apartment. I returned the now-automatic Persian politesse: "May God watch over you."

My run-in, so to speak, with the *komiteh* had been a good distraction. Somehow I felt cleansed. My deep sadness had shifted. For several nights my mother, the family bard, packed our living room with guests anxious to hear the famous story. By the fourth or fifth time that she repeated it, I almost believed that the *komiteh* had put handcuffs on me and had thrown me violently into the backseat of their police vehicle. My mother imitated the faux phone call I would have had to make, begging my elderly parents to save me from the customary eighty lashes. That part consistently drew the biggest laughs. In the end, I suppose it was a worthwhile experience for all the merriment it produced. We could all use a little more laughter in this life.

Are you laughing much these days?

Love,
Jasmine

December 15, 1997

Dear Dot,

I awoke to a child's voice screaming and crying and had to reorient myself to where I was. After a typically huge lunch meal of okra stew over saffron-steamed rice and lamb bathed in spinach and plum sauce, I had actually succumbed to the siesta. I was at my cousin Fariba's house, making the relative rounds. Each one was anxious to show me their affection through lavish meals, as if they could stuff me with love. Fariba's eight-year-old daughter, Afsoon, interrupted our peace and quiet with her shrieks. Apparently, her older brother, Kamran, had released her pet chick into the alley, and it was nowhere to be found. Kamran was a mischievous child who often bothered his younger sister.

"Why do you insist on hurting your sister?" my cousin yelled at her son, holding him by the shoulders and shaking him, as if the answer would fall out. Unfortunately, the boy could not bring himself to apologize.

"Because she is a bad girl with all your spoiling."

"I will tell you who the rotten one is around here: you. And this is what you get for being nasty." Fariba spanked her son a few times and sent him to the cellar to do his crying.

I cried with him. Corporal punishment was nothing new. While time-outs were my preferred form of disciplining, I knew children were still spanked in the States, if less openly than in Iran. Why was I reacting so strongly to this episode? Did I feel sorry for Kamran? Not really. He was cruel to his sister and her beloved pet. He deserved to be punished. So, what was it?

I remembered spanking Aria, a year before her death. I know I must have told you about it as I was traumatized for days afterward. Katie McGovern and Aria were watching *Sesame Street* in the den. I was in the kitchen making the girls a snack. I hummed to myself, content with domesticity. It was not often that I returned home from work early enough to let Aria invite a friend over, even if only a neighbor. I distinctly remember feeling at peace with my position in the world as I placed each raisin atop the peanut-butter-covered celery sticks.

When I returned to the den to serve the girls their snack, I could not find them. "Girls!" I yelled, waiting for them to emerge from their hiding place. "Come out now!" I searched the bathroom. There was no sign of them. "You are not being funny anymore. Girls, I demand you show yourselves this instant!" Finally, I saw the partially opened screen door. Had I left the door ajar? Terrible images passed through my mind. I started to panic.

I called the McGovern house: no sign of them. Eleanor tried to calm me down. I patrolled the neighborhood: nothing. I was on the phone with a police officer when I heard their giggling through the back door. I dropped the phone in the midst of conversation and confirmed what I heard. It was true. I saw them: each held a can of Cherry Coke in her hands. They had walked to the grocery store a few blocks away. I was not sure how the girls accessed money, nor how a clerk had accepted their cash without being suspicious, but there they were.

"What in the hell did you think you were doing?" I screamed at Aria. She started to cry. I had never before used harsh words with her nor such a violent tone.

"Okay, Mama," she pleaded. "Time-out for a whole week."

"Forget it. Do not ever leave the house without telling me again, get it?"

I spanked her bottom just as Eleanor walked in. Just once and not very hard, but it terrified me, I think, more than it did her. I had fallen into the trap of my own childhood. Aria was likely more shocked by the fact that I had hit her than from the pain of the spank. She ran into her room, where I heard her burst into tears again. By that time Eleanor was dragging Katie home, trying to avoid more of our scene. When I finally calmed down, I explained to her how much she had frightened me. She kissed me on the nose and promised never again.

Seeing Kamran spanked made me realize how quickly I have suppressed the bad memories of Aria. I fear that I am forgetting what she was really like. She was a wonderful child, but she was far from perfect. Perfection is for angels, and I worry that angel is what she is becoming for me now.

My cousin Fariba wants to know what am I doing here in Iran and how long I plan to stay. Why do I care so much about these old family stories? Giving me volumes of free, unsolicited advice as if it were her birthright, she and all my relatives here feel a certain entitlement to know exactly what I am thinking and doing.

"I am like that lost chick in the alley," I replied. "Lost, alone, and trying to find my way home."

I think about you all the time, dear friend. How your friendship has helped make a home for me in America. I do not know when I will return. But you will be the first to know.

Love,
Jasmine

January 1, 1998

Dear Dot,

I am in the crowded Tehran bazaar, a maze of narrow covered passages, a city within a city, and find myself hunting for Aria's face. It is almost impossible not to get lost in here. The shops all look alike and are organized by common theme: gold, silver, dishes, old copper and brassware, shoes, clothes, spices and other dried goods, handmade rugs and saddlebags. There are mosques, guesthouses, and banks along the route. The lighting is dim, a glass porthole from the vaulted ceiling, and the architecture not nearly as nice as the photos I have seen of the historic bazaars in Shiraz and Esfahan. I could have sworn I saw Aria behind a tall bag of eucalyptus leaves. I wove through the cacophony of constant hammering, vendors shouting to recruit customers, and even the occasional donkey hauling in goods to search for my girl, only to get more lost.

Those of us who follow the Gregorian calendar have entered a new year, but here, in Iran, it is just another day in the year 1376 (marking the start of Prophet Muhammad's pilgrimage from Mecca to Medina). Over ten months without Aria, and still, somewhere in the recesses of my subconscious self, I hold out hope.

Perhaps even more preposterous was my five-hour drive last week over steep, treacherous roads to visit the healer, Sheikh Abdollah, in his mountain village. How is it that I can have such a skeptical and scientific mind and yet turn to fortune-tellers and shamans? The truth is that I am desperate to dream about her. Each morning I relive the disappointment. Why have I been denied this reunion with my daughter? Nothing has been of help to overcome this problem, so who else to turn to but those purportedly in touch with the other side?

The Sheikh ignored my mission and instead told me irrelevant stories, like the one about the nightingale's love affair with the rose. My mother later informed me that it is a classic folktale. In Iran nightingales supposedly sing to the roses with such rapture that they lose their senses. In this stupor, they are easy prey for the prowling cats. The Sheikh asked me a strange question: Did I think the nightingale should sing? How should I know? What relevance did this have to the issue at hand? I was frustrated by his lack of transparency and his inability to address my concerns, so I ignored the question and instead reiterated my desire to have him help me dream about my dead child. In the end, we did not understand each other. He gave me a kind of consolation prize, an amulet of a turquoise eye with a beady black pupil. It was the kind that you can buy in any five-and-dime store here. I am supposed to wear it around my neck at all times to avert *cheshmeh-bad,* the evil eye. Despite my annoyance at the way he treated me, I wear it.

I tried once again to manipulate my dreams so that Aria would make an appearance. This last attempt was with a bona fide psychic, known simply as Sir Doctor (apparently he had a Ph.D. in child psychology). Fortunately, the trip was not nearly as arduous as visiting the Sheikh. I awaited the doctor-psychic at the home of Mina Naini, a childhood friend whose father had a visiting professorship at Cal in 1967. Mina and her family live in an upscale northern Tehran neighborhood tucked in the base of the Elburz Mountains.

Tara and Sara, Mina's two teenage girls, insisted we precede Sir Doctor's arrival by watching their favorite new video: *As Good as It Gets.* The girls were disappointed that I had not even heard of the film. They were entrenched in the love story between an acid-tongued, obsessive-compulsive romance novelist (played by Jack Nicholson) and the beautiful, resilient, single-mother waitress (played by Helen Hunt) and had already watched the film four or five times. Only the occasional unveiled head obstructing the scene and the inappropriate sneeze revealed its counterfeit origins, likely an illegal videotaping of the film in a U.S. movie theater. Jack Nicholson and Helen Hunt would be amused to know how popular they are among Iranian cinema fans, how their film had spread like wildfire through an Islamic Republic where VCRs were officially banned, but most people skirted the law.

Tara and Sara were highly entertaining between their contraband fashion magazines smuggled in by Iranian friends living in Europe, their obsession with Madonna and the Spice Girls, and their tennis lessons in whites in a gym for women only that allowed them to unveil in privacy. Their Persian was interspersed with attempts at English slang: "Wow!" they say sounding more like "Vow," or "Top" they respond when something was high quality. My personal favorite was "Ouch!" which they use when something was expensive. Tara, the seventeen-year-old, told me she planned to have a nose job next year. Sara, two years younger, showed me her cellular phone and was visibly disheartened when she learned that I called it a cell phone instead of a "mobile" (which she pronounced as "mobeel"). The West has been cut off from post-Revolution Iran, but obviously the reverse was not true.

It was the girls' idea that I consult Sir Doctor about my dreaming problem. Tara and Sara persuaded their parents to make the appointment with the psychic five months ago. It was the latest fad to hit the chic neighborhoods of northern Tehran. "The government wants to pick his brain first and then throw him into jail," said Tara. "They are afraid of him and what he might say about the future of our Islamic Revolution," echoed Sara. "His phone number changes every two weeks. When we called to make an appointment, we had to use code words before his secretary would even speak to us."

Sir Doctor appeared exactly on time. He was in his seventies, with snowy hair and a gray suit that matched his eyes. He did not wear a tie, that symbol of Western orientation, but carried with him a black leather briefcase, making him look much more like a business professional than a psychic. He said a quiet, but respectful *"Salaam"* and was quickly whisked away into the living room, where he could have privacy with each of those who sought his counsel. We sat in the television room barely watching the film, whispering with anticipation as we awaited each person's return from the living room. Apparently, Sir Doctor had uncanny talent. After a few seconds of looking into a person's eyes, he could write down their full name and birth date, and even the names of their family members. He could also name future spouses and children, which is what sent the girls into a tizzy. Even I was caught up in their excitement.

I was the last to be invited by Sir Doctor into the living room. "I am very sorry, Dr. Talahi," he said to me before I had a chance to greet him. "Perhaps this is a waste of your time. I am incapable of doing dream implantations." He had a soft, soothing voice fitting for a therapist or fortune-teller, or an oncologist for that matter. He looked into my eyes only briefly. "What a shame about Aria's accident." I was sure one of the girls had told him my situation. I nodded my head, no longer jarred by receiving condolences about Aria. It was a daily occurrence in Iran.

"Listen," he said. "I know that Aria's death has made you doubt everything, and that you have lost the certainty you once had." I nodded again. None of his comments moved me nor belonged exclusively to the realm of psychics. "I am here to tell you that coming to Iran was the right decision, even if your long departure makes your . . ." He stopped for a second and wrote Alexander in perfect Latin script. "Eskandar is how we would say it in our language. Yes, your Eskandar suffers so much in your absence." Then Sir Doctor looked at me with a half smile, as if he knew this would startle me and validate his unusual powers. Of course he was right. I started to shake, for no one in Iran had heard of Alexander. Since I had already been condemned for living with Justin and having a baby out of wedlock, I was not going to add more fuel to the fire by talking about Alex. "Aria has sent you to Iran, my dear. Only by finding out who you are and where you come from can you understand the deep sadness you carry around like a pregnancy."

He smiled at me then, with the perfect, pearly white teeth possible only in dentures. "My advice to you, my dear lady doctor, is to learn how to live within the doubt, but to also recognize what is undeniably true. In Iran you have drawn upon the strength of your grandmother to heal your relationship with your parents and have opened your heart unlike ever before. Let yourself love this Eskandar again."

Sir Doctor abruptly stood up and walked toward the other room. Our time together had apparently expired. Mina's husband handed him the money, in a neat stack of bills held in place by a rubber band. The psychic walked to the door and turned to address us one final time before his departure: "My role in this world is to warn people of what is to come and to give them a sense of peace by diminishing their fears. I hope I have done this for all of you this afternoon. May God always be with you."

"What happened in there?" asked Mina. "Your face is the color of chalk."

"He told me that Aria sent me to Iran, but that I must return soon to my life in America."

Mina's eyes got wet. "He really is something. I swear upon the tombstone of my father that none of us told him anything about you."

Perhaps Sir Doctor is telepathic, a highly intuitive reader of minds. Or maybe some member of Mina's family apprised him of my story only to maintain a perfect poker face. Whatever the explanation, I found solace in his advice and admiration in his skill. Meanwhile, I continue cataloging my heritage with new passion and purpose, despite an ongoing failure to dream about Aria. There is so much more to learn here before I am ready to return to Seattle.

Love,
Jasmine

January 24, 1998

Dear Dot,

It was so good to talk with you last night. Thank you for splurging on a phone call for my birthday. It was the best gift you could have given me. I received Alexander's card today, a stunning photograph he took of moonlight bouncing off a nineteenth-century Japanese stone lamp with the caption, "My love, wishing you a year of light after so much darkness."

Another year has passed despite my futile wish that time would freeze to a year ago. What carefree joy we experienced during my last birthday with that hilarious Persian dance video you bought for me of that hairy-chested Tehrangeles Richard Simmons in a leotard. You were so precious smiling demurely between flirtatious flicks of your wrist. Do you remember how hard we laughed as Alex moved his eyebrows up and down with each undulation of his hip? How amazed we were that Aria could naturally jiggle her shoulders in that Khuzestani dance?

I am finally living in the here and now. Only occasionally do I escape to my memories. My menstrual cycle, as if on cue, has started up again after six months of hibernation. I must admit, a part of me fantasized about being pregnant again. Having been a mother now, I realize that most women probably get pregnant without having a clue how their lives will change. Perhaps all the myths about feeling wonderful during pregnancy are needed to perpetuate the human race. We reproduce with a blind faith that everything will turn out for the best. We do not hear about how we will be derailed by motherhood, how we will second-guess ourselves as parents, that every tragic event we hear on the news will haunt us ten times more imagining what the mothers of the deceased are going through. The hemorrhoids and heartburn, the weight gain and disfigurement, the permanent stretch marks and C-section scars are nothing compared to the vulnerability that persists for life.

I cannot imagine what it feels like to be a father. I was once Daddy's girl, but as I grew to school-aged, my interactions with Baba became focused on my education. He was obsessed with my grades, as if they alone measured all of his success in the new country. Thankfully, I never disappointed him on this front. My studies seemed to be our only topic of conversation. He never interfered with my activities outside of school, nor knew how to comfort me beyond buying me gifts. The personal sphere became solely my mother's domain.

Baba does not know what to make of my newfound interest in our family history. He seems nervous to hear me digging through Mamani Joon's history. When I asked him about Mamani Joon's first love, Tamas, he was visibly annoyed. "*Dokhtaram,* why do you fill your mind with such nonsense? Have the women been embellishing their tales again?" I approached him another way.

"Baba, did you ever feel like Mamani Joon was in love with your Baba Joon?"

"Such a Western question, my child. Falling in love sounds romantic, but it is nothing but pure propaganda."

I have decided to accompany my father on one of his trips to Khuzestan. On the fifteen-hour drive southwest, I know we will talk mostly about politics, his business dealings, and medical complaints. But my secret hope is that in visiting the desert oasis of his childhood, I will have a context for his stories, get to know him better, and restore our deep, early connection.

Love,
Jasmine

TELEGRAM

To: Jasmine Talahi

From: Dot Wilkins & Alexander Forsythe

Date: February 17, 1998

Dearest J, Volumes of responses to yr letters but must be brief. Can it be one year already? According to papyrus from Greco-Roman period, dwarfs protect dead! Greek mythology also recognizes yr grandmother's fruit. Persephone's pomegranate symbolizes promise of spring after descent to world of dead. Alex found pomegranate imported from Israel + we smashed it against yr threshold like modern Athenians—not so different from yr outburst last year. Was full of seeds = good omen. Means your spirit will persist despite forces dragging toward underworld + abundant luck (u r long overdue). We trust this newfound hope 4 this year & blessings from ancient sources. Love U, Dot & Alex

February 17, 1998

Dear Dottie and Alexander,

There is an official mourning ceremony here for the one-year anniversary of Aria's death. People in Iran may miss a wedding, but it is virtually unheard of to not make a presence at the fortieth day and the one-year mark postmortem. It is an important ritual, a grand production, and not a modest expense. The women in my family have been working hard in the kitchen for days. The menu: saffron and yogurt baked rice with chicken, skewers of lamb kebabs marinated in special spices, pitchers of *dough* (a minty yogurt drink), rosewater fritters and saffron pudding for dessert. Excess food will go to the poor, a *nazry* offering encouraged by Islamic tradition.

The usual protocol is grand-scale grieving for seven days after a death. There is the memorial service on day three (*khatm*), the one-week remembrance (*hafteh*), followed by anniversaries on the fortieth day (*cheleh*) and one year (*sal*) later. Thursdays are cemetery days, preceding Friday prayer and the day of rest. Those closest to the dead visit the grave site each week, watering the trees around it, washing the gravestone, emptying their hearts.

For today's *sal,* there is a professional crier for the women's group. The men have their own ritual in a house separate from where the women are gathered, not surprising given the everyday level of sexual segregation here: on buses, in schools, movie theaters, and mosques. The crier is like an emcee for mourning. She begins with a song that I do not understand, but within thirty seconds of singing, the room is filled with a steady rhythm of sobbing. There is a crescendo of sounds, some from the back of the throat, others from deep in the belly. Women I have met for the first time in my life rip their collars, slap their thighs, claw their faces, seem to convulse in grief at the loss of my daughter.

My first instinct is to ridicule every one of them for taking part in this theater of the absurd, this grieving marathon. I want to scream at their excoriated faces: "How can you be suffering for the loss of my daughter, *my* daughter." Except that, somehow, their empathy seems sincere. The crying is contagious. Despite my initial composure, I join in the tears. The truth is we are all crying for our own reasons, for there is no shortage of grief.

The crier senses a climax in the grieving and punctuates her song with a funny story about a Christian missionary. We all laugh through our tears, a break in the tension. Then there is more choreographed crying: for the Iranian child who will never see Iran, for the grandparents who will never know their grandchild, for the mother who is left childless. Twenty minutes later, on her way out the door, the crier cups my face with her hands and says, "Remember, my child, silent grief is dangerous for the soul."

The eating and socializing start up again. After the intense physical and emotional release of this afternoon, the mood is quite festive. The children go outside for a soccer game in the alley. A backgammon and card game competition have started among the men, informs a young boy cousin who can still move with ease between the two worlds. Over tea we gather on the cushions, gossiping like schoolgirls. One woman tells a sexual joke.

These days I question everything, especially myself. What part of me finds truth in this ancient culture? What exactly is my culture anyway? In the States we have such public boundaries for grief and most other life-changing experiences. A single memorial service is supposed to be sufficient to recognize the feelings of loss. These hushed, reverential rituals have denied me the intensity and multiple layers of my grief. I smiled with recognition at your Greek practice. You both understand. Like the pomegranate, we have been broken open and need to stay in this state if we have any chance of recovering. Iran is a country where censorship is commonplace, behavior that threatens religious values is publicly suppressed, and women are veiled, but the expression of emotion is loud, unapologetic, and chaotic. There is no squelching of passion here. We cry as long as we need to.

Love,
Persephone Awaiting Spring

March 11, 1998

Dear Dot,

Persian New Year, Norouz, is the first day of spring. This biggest and most joyous holiday in Iran has its roots in Zoroastrian times thousands of years ago. As implied by its synchrony with the vernal equinox, this is a celebration of renewal and rebirth, jettisoning the darkness of winter for the new blossoms of spring. For the last couple of weeks, Iranians have been engaged in a kind of spring cleaning: washing their carpets, rearranging their homes, making new clothes, baking pastries, and germinating seeds.

In a week from today, the last Wednesday of the year, our family will go to a small park outside of the city to light bonfires and leap over their flames. Even my mother will do the ceremonial jump, shouting the traditional words to exchange the pain and pallor of the preceding year with the healthy redness of the coming one. I have been helping Maman with her ceremonial New Year cloth, *sofreh-e haft cinn,* the seven items starting with the Persian letter for *S.* Each item is either a celebration of life or symbolizes an important wish for the coming year (wisdom, health, good fortune, etc.). Setting a beautiful *sofreh* is a family tradition I hope to continue myself.

We had recovered from Aria's *sal.* Our relatives were busy with preparations for the new year. Baba was busy in the bazaar, and Maman and I finally had uninterrupted time to ourselves. While I was rearranging the fuchsia hyacinth, Maman was chatting away with me, adding photographs of our dead beloveds to the *sofreh.* Then she did something that stopped our conversation in midsentence. She added a small photo album called "Aria: My Grandbaby."

I remembered sending Maman and Baba Aria's birth announcement. I was hoping the sweet newborn photo of their grandchild still looking slightly cone-headed would win them over. Looking back on it now, I can see how doing that was counterproductive and antagonistic. After all, my mother had begged me not to become pregnant without marrying Justin, and I was still too insulted by her letter to admit that we had in fact planned to get married. I could not bring myself to tell them that Justin had died, as if his ruptured aneurysm would validate their opinions of his weakness, God's way of saying I got what I deserved for betraying them. When they never responded to my news and continued to enforce their silence, I never sent them word of my daughter again.

I opened Maman's album, white with gold around the edges. In it were dozens of photos of Aria: her kindergarten photos, birthday pictures, Aria dressed as a pumpkin at Halloween, and the two of us in a haystack in the Forsythe barn in Platte. The album was not limited to photos: There were drawings, handprints, Justin's obituary, and even a copy of a certificate signed by Mr. Saito in honor of Aria's completion of *Suzuki Violin Book 1.* Aria's obituary was conspicuously absent.

You were the only person capable of sending such documentation of Aria. I was stunned. How could you have done this without informing me? I thought we had no secrets between us. I could not decide whether I was furious or hurt, thankful or relieved, before my mother interrupted my thoughts.

"I used to worry why your closest friend was an accident of nature, a poor, deformed thing. It made me wonder: Is that how my daughter feels too? Is she a broken human being who needs company? I thought and thought about it, until I came to the conclusion that you felt as out of place as Hasan and me, lost between two countries and cultures. Maybe your attraction to this dwarf had to do with finding someone who understood your confusion and failure to belong.

"We thought we had done such a good job raising you. You were always so smart and accomplished, Yasaman Joon. At one point Hasan said to me, 'Maryam, all this misery you and I are going through to live in this cursed country has been worthwhile. Our daughter has succeeded. She has reached our highest aspirations.' He was referring to all your honors and top grades, and your early acceptance to medical school.

"He did not know what I knew: that you had lost yourself to this good-for-nothing boy with no future. One night I heard you talking with him on the phone, and I realized: This was not the Yasaman I had raised! All this time I fooled myself into believing I was your best friend and confidante. After that episode, each time you went into your room, I made a practice of picking up the phone to learn more about this daughter I no longer knew. I was horrified by what I heard and disgusted. The way he talked to you, it was clear there was no sense of respect for your body or mind. Saddest of all was that you did not seem to respect yourself either.

"I was almost certain you had engaged in the most intimate of acts with him, and I spent nights tossing and turning in bed trying to rationalize my way out of that awful image. I kicked myself for letting you live in the dormitory, for not keeping a closer eye on you. Then my worst nightmare came true. It confirmed everything I had suspected but nothing I wanted to admit: You were pregnant. Thanks to God, you had the sense to go on with your education and abort the child." My jaw dropped. I remained mute.

"The day you went to the abortion clinic is the day I knew your friend Dottie was worthy of you after all. It was she who accompanied you through this dishonorable experience, not the hateful boy. I sat in a taxi in the parking lot and watched the two of you enter the clinic. I was listening to all of your phone conversations by then and heard you mention the date and place to Dottie. That dog of a man, may God rot his soul, did not even have the decency to accompany you there, to say nothing about paying for the operation. Of course the taxi came from a different company than Hasan's. Can you imagine how ashamed I would have been if your father had found out about all this? I sent the taxi driver away for a couple of hours, promising to pay him whatever he wanted for his time.

"She held your hand and looked at you with such love that I started to cry. I wanted to be the one you turned to for the horrible events in your life, but to admit that I knew you were having sex with a man before marriage was far more shame than I could handle. I could not encourage your immoral behaviors and prayed that this humiliating experience would teach you to respect yourself in the future.

"I saw you exiting the clinic and was shocked by what I saw. I had expected to see my daughter looking physically or emotionally beaten up. I was so relieved to see you walking normally that I could have kissed the dirty steering wheel in thanks. Meanwhile, you threw yourself into your last term of courses at Berkeley. I, on the other hand, went into a deep depression. I thought you were safe at the Harvard of the West. I could not accept that my little girl who I loved more than life itself was no different than those American whores. How many times had I told you that giving away your sacred curtain to any man but your husband would be the worst mistake of your life?

"I could not sleep, had no interest in food, and refused to be touched by your father. Hasan, the poor soul, was clueless about all this, but he did notice my depression. He thought my sadness had to do with missing my family and tiring of this hard and lonely American life. I remember writing a long letter to my sister, your aunt Fereshteh, admitting my misery, though not the real reasons for it. She confessed later how surprised she had been by this news. She had received nothing but cheerful letters about our new life in

America, the mythical land of promise. She knew all about your wonderful successes and believed we had a house befitting a sultan, with swimming pool and large courtyard garden. We had continued to send money home on a regular basis, sustaining these visions of a pretend good life, even as we suffered financially ourselves. If only my sister knew that we lived not far from the urban low class, in a neighborhood full of Chinese and Mexicans, pretending to make a happy life among all the other struggling immigrant families.

"Later, when we returned to Iran, I told her about the real America. How most of the people have icy hearts, how they seem very nice at first but are rarely willing to be true friends. I told her how they worked us like mules, with so little time to spend with our loved ones. Neither Hasan nor I could ever come home for lunch, and we were lucky if we dined together two or three times a week. I talked about the violence in the streets: the drugs, the men with long hair, and the fact that people could carry guns and be shot for no good reason. I detailed the arrogance and ignorance of most Americans. Most of them did not even know where Iran was, and when they did, they assumed we rode camels and lacked basic technology like televisions.

"Years before you changed into an American girl, your grandmother had felt all of these things too. She talked to me on many occasions about returning home to Iran. She would have left long before she did if it were not for you. You were her only granddaughter, the cherished only child of her eldest son. But there were other grandchildren in Tehran and

Khuzestan. She had an obligation to them too, even if she favored you above the rest. Hasan was so stressed from our financial situation that he could not begin to consider letting our source of child care leave, even as he knew how much his mother suffered. Tahereh Joon, God rest her soul, begged me for a solution. In fact, she was the one who came up with the community center idea. It was a brilliant idea, and, *joony,* I think you inherited all of your intelligence from your grandmother. Hasan had no choice but to send her back home after hearing that she spat in my face. Of course, it was all make-believe. My mother-in-law and I were deep allies, even if we occasionally squabbled about household affairs.

"We left you shortly after your Berkeley graduation. I wanted to be proud of all your honors, the way your baba was, but I was drowning in images of you sinning with that stupid boy. I thought about taking you with us to Iran, making you give up your entry to UCSF medical school. Hasan reminded me that your Farsi was no better than elementary school level and that you could not become a doctor so easily in Iran.

"The day I found out about your pregnancy was the loneliest day of my life. I realized that I had lost my baby *joon* to America, no matter if she was pure Iranian in her blood. I thought about hiring a top gynecologist in Iran to sew you back up so that no man would know the difference. After all, what respectable groom would accept a defiled woman? But then I knew you would never go along with this plan, you who were probably proud of your deflowering.

"In Iran I was a much happier person, so my constant worrying about you did not reveal itself as much. At first we scraped together all our money to visit you every couple of years. There was a rift between us now, but neither you nor Hasan seemed to notice. I could hide my disappointment during our short visits. I had given up all hopes of guiding your life back toward us. I knew I no longer had any control.

"Eight years ago Hasan decided we should call our daughter at the first minute of Norouz. It was six in the morning your time, and who do you think picked up the phone? That Justin fellow with his head still in dreamland. He said hello and then handed the phone to you. My daughter, you did not even have the decency to pretend it was a wrong number! You should have made excuses, denied the fact that your boyfriend was spending the night with you, but instead you left no way out for yourself but banishment from the family. Hasan slammed down the phone and cursed you for weeks. His New Year was ruined. You wrote us a letter explaining yourself like a stupid and straightforward American girl, that you were in love with this average-joe teacher and that he had already moved in with you. You thought you might marry him someday, but he had such a bitter taste in his mouth from his parents' divorce that he was hesitant to make that commitment just yet. Now there was no chance of having a relationship with you. Hasan forbade me from calling or writing again, although I defied him to send you a long letter a few months later. Of course he was not the only one who was furious. *Dokhtaram,* what came over you then? At least you had the sense to try to keep your abortion a secret. What were you thinking when you admitted to your elderly, traditional father that you were in fact no better than a prostitute, living with a man to whom you were not married?

"Your friend, the little one, she was good enough to send me evidence of my granddaughter, but I did not dare to respond. Hasan refused to let me reestablish contact with you, even though looking at these pictures of your little Aria melted my heart. I was ashamed for the way I had pitied Dottie on so many occasions. Now she was doing me this biggest favor of my life. I felt so guilty, and each year made a *nazry* donation to the organization for handicapped children in Iran, the place that helped rehabilitate all of the dwarfs in our country. Dottie sent me those packages with warm notes reassuring me that you and Aria were doing well, encouraging me to call you or pay a visit. Our *khanoom postchee,* the kind woman who worked in the post office, knew she was delivering something precious from America just from the look in my eyes. Every few months she graced our door with news of you and Aria Joon. Without your little friend, without this *khanoom postchee,* I would have surely gone mad.

"Now it is almost exactly twenty-one years since I realized you were no longer my little girl, that I had failed to teach you the honorable ways of the world, that you were no different from those low-class girls I had criticized a million times to your face. I have sorrow every day just thinking

> about this. It has hurt me so much not to see you or have contact with you. You were my jewel. You gave my life purpose. But these terrible things I endured are nothing compared to what you have suffered. Your baba and I have lived through revolution, war, the loss of our fortunes, and separation from our only child. But it is nothing like the pain you must feel after Aria's death. At least I knew you were alive and well. Even if I did not speak to you, I never felt distant from you, partly in thanks to your little friend."

Then Maman crumbled like I had never seen before. No longer capable of speaking, she pulled me close.

"Maman, I was so mad at you and Baba for abandoning me after Berkeley. I was not even a full adult then. I needed you. I missed you so much. But you were never able to accept me for who I was. You always wanted me to be more Iranian, but the truth is, I have only ever been American. When all these bad things kept happening in my life, in the back of my mind I always wondered if I was being punished for straying from your standards. I know that you always wanted the best for me. I am so sorry for keeping you far away." Then I started to sob too. Maman rocked me as if I were a young child. Perhaps she envisioned me as that seven-year-old, in deep need of her comfort after Mamani Joon's departure, or maybe she fantasized it was Aria in her arms. We never talked about these stories again. However, like rosewater added to a pastry, the traces of it were always present.

Thanks to you, my mother never lost touch with her only grandchild. You naughty girl! How you shocked me with those secret letters to Maman. In the final analysis, I am so grateful for your covert actions. Thank you, dear friend, for seeing beyond my limitations and having the courage to act upon it.

When I brought the last Norouz item to the *sofreh,* I asked Maman why we included *serkeh* (vinegar). "*Serkeh* represents age and patience," Maman informed me. As you would say, thank the goddess for both.

Love you,
Jazz

March 9, 1998

Dearest Jasmine,

Here's hoping this card reaches you in time to wish you a happy Norouz. I've heard that the Taliban will ban New Year's celebrations in Afghanistan this year—a damn shame. I remember the coming of spring in the Hindu Kush as so festive, even during wartime. Your Norouz has been celebrated by all the major cultures of ancient Mesopotamia, as far back as the Sumerians in 3000 B.C. The funny thing is, for just as long, it continues to be the target of animosity by foreign invaders and anti-national forces. Alexander the Great, the Arab conquerors, and others tried to wipe off the holiday of the Persian Empire, only to find it preserved by the masses.

I don't know how the hell it's possible that a whole year has gone by since Aria last walked this earth and you left to circle it. My friends at the bereavement group warn me that time is a false friend. So it doesn't surprise me at all that you feel like you take two steps forward one day and one step back the next. I feel that way myself, although the general trend is looking better.

I'm in Boston this week, for my twenty-fifth college reunion. I wish you were here with me. Somehow, I've forgotten to bring my camera on this trip. Truth be told, a picture only captures the fiction of a single moment—everything is subject to change. Calvin, never one to censor his thoughts, was only too glad to hear about my trip. "You know what this means, Forsythe?" he said, punching me in the arm, a half-smoked cigarette behind his ear. "Son, you're making progress! You're no longer hovering around that fax machine waiting for her microscopic handwriting blurred from God-knows-where to transmit. You're not even logging on to the Internet every five minutes like a goddamn obsessive compulsive in case she's sent you an e-mail from Siberia! This is progress, I say! It's about time!" He slapped me on the back a couple times. God bless him—I know he's looking after me in his own way.

I'm not in a mood to socialize—not sure exactly what I'm doing here. So I took a walk over lunch through the Back Bay. I came upon a memorial for the nine firefighters killed on June 17, 1972, in the old Hotel Vendôme. You know I'm not usually into memorial art, but these things hit me differently now. There's a dark panel shaped like a sea-horse spine, draped by a bronze fireman's jacket and hat, the names of each firefighter engraved. The memorial tells the story of the tragic fire and quotes the survivors. I sat for a moment on the facing bench, not sure why I was obsessing over the names, when I came upon this simple quote that made me think of us: "Sometimes you have to say, there's nothing more we could've done."

On my walk back to the library, I took Newbury Street, the chichi Rodeo Drive equivalent in this provincial city. I passed the Ritz-Carlton, Burberry's, the Versace store, and Giorgio Armani. I thought of you as I passed Berkeley Street, and then my eye caught a small sign informing the public that the Gallery NAGA was open. I don't know what compelled me to enter, but I decided to check out the paintings of Robert Ferrandini.

His paintings were incredible—trees of various shapes, sizes, and colors are the protagonists of his work. They sit in serene landscapes, wisps of clouds or islands floating about in dim lighting a romantic could take for a perpetual sunset.

After looking closely at the faded beauty of these scenes, I began seeing layers of images beneath the trees, landscapes, and skies. I felt like Dot excavating paintings beneath paintings. There was a rock shadow here, an empty wineglass there, tree skeletons hidden in the clouds. This was a painter who rewrote his own history.

In his painting called *The Lives of the Saints,* ten trees framing the painting move from ground to sky. Each tree has its own personality—there are elements of hilarity and sacredness in each of them. One is bright orange, another electric blue; the yellow one is dainty, the brown one imposing, but all are rootless. It suddenly became clear to me that these free-floating trees, reproduced in every painting, were Ferrandini's ghosts or, rather, his way of expressing persistent loss. With every brush stroke on each branch, he tries to re-create what is no longer tangibly there until at last it transcends this life.

I haven't told you yet about the painting that calls your name. In *The Garden of Allah,* there are trees that are perfectly straight, painted in fine detail like a Persian miniature. Again, you can see the ghost trees in the background. Beside this bucolic scene, there is a series of angry dark blue waves. I imagine it to be the Caspian Sea, foaming with Persian calligraphy that I will never be able to decipher. This painting is the perfected calm of your outer weather, my darling, and the ferocious storm inside you.

I sit and I sketch it over and over again. There's so much intimacy in this act, in our shared history. I may never touch the rough sea within you, just as you may not understand my unquestioning faith in us, but it's not the end of the world. There's room for an incommunicado element in our love, distance in our grieving.

I saw a photo of Robert Ferrandini in the catalog. He has a gaunt Italian face dominated by large glasses that are tinted rose, as if he can't bear to look at the world unfiltered. Despite the subdued light, the skeletons of other paintings in the background, and the trees that hold grieving branches, you also get a sense of hope in the lifting of his clouds. In spite of his suffering, Ferrandini took a stab at creating beauty. He—like me, like you—has been forced to redesign himself, and with hard work and soul-searching, he's made it.

I see you everywhere, Jasmine—in paintings, memorials, and even at this boring reunion. May this Persian New Year bring you closer to peace and whatever else you need to do to return home.

Love,
Alexander

April 29, 1998

Dear Dot,

Today I attended a *taziyeh,* the direct translation of which is "consolation." It is a passion play, an elaborate pageant that memorializes the martyrdom of Imam Husayn, beloved grandson of the Prophet. Martyrdom is an important and unfortunately familiar concept in the Islamic Republic, where it is venerated as a shortcut to Heaven. Mothers who have lost their sons in the Iran-Iraq war (the most current source of martyrs, numbering over a quarter of a million) are supposed to be joyful because it means automatic paradise for their beloveds in the afterlife. There are parks covered with red tulips (the symbol of the martyr and the national flower of Iran), large billboards in busy intersections in praise of a martyr's holiness, television shows exalting the life of these martyrs, special privileges for the children of martyrs, and even a martyr museum. A common expression of affection, *ghorbanat beram,* literally translated means "I would martyr myself for you."

The basic story line of the *taziyeh* is this: On his way to contesting his hereditary right to the caliphate, Husayn was murdered in Karbala, in southern Iraq, along with all of his compatriots and male children. His female entourage was taken hostage, a fate considered worse than death. For Shiites, this is the ultimate example of divine sacrifice, the acme of suffering. By enacting this grand conflict, the Muslims of Iran not only pay tribute to one of their favorite imams, but they become part of the continuous struggle for justice against evil.

These *taziyehs* are grand mourning celebrations (if such words can be put together) dating back to the mid-eighteenth century, but it is not the history of the event that captured my attention. Like the crucifixion of Christ, what happens to Husayn is tragic, but it feels too remote and mythical to move me. I am still trying to figure out how the drama of an imam and his clan killed in 680 A.D. translates into present-day emotions.

The director stood with the actors on a round platform in a grassy knoll beside the mosque. He gave cues during the performance, helping inexperienced actors take their positions, and moving props, which were as simple as a basin of water to symbolize the Euphrates River or a tree branch approximating an entire palm grove. The performers (all men, veiled women are easy to impersonate) ran on- and offstage, weaving their way through the audience, announcing where they were going and from where they had arrived. The "good Muslims," dressed in green, sang their parts, while the enemy, in red (symbolizing blood and cruelty), shrieked and chanted like buffoons. Only a few memorized their lines. The majority read from tiny folded scripts in their palms.

This amateur performance had emotional results for the audience. Even my educated, modern cousins shed tears. It started with soldiers and relatives dying in Husayn's arms. Three hours later, a two-person lion with a black flag in its mouth stood guard over the dead bodies in Karbala, including that of Husayn's, and the sobs reached their zenith. These were real tears, from men and women alike, though the children were less likely to be crying. The level of emotion at this *taziyeh* was supposedly subdued compared to others that take place during Ashura, the height of this Islamic month of Muharram dedicated to mourning. Ashura, only eight days away, brings processions of men flagellating themselves with steel balls and chains with blades, creating real bruises and even drawing blood.

To many in the Western world, the theatricality of grief and self-immolation sound absurd. Of course, not everyone in Iran relates to it either. Tara and Sara refer to *taziyehs* as "Husayn parties." It is one of the few chances these girls have to socialize with boys in public, without the objections of the moral police. They smile through their false tears, accepting notes with phone numbers from the sweaty palms of flirtatious young men.

For the most part, grief is a normal part of life here. The children are not spared from it; indeed, they are raised within it. Those who did not shed a tear at the *taziyeh* in their youth will probably do so when they have come to know real pain. Though my first reaction to the *taziyeh* was to mock it, the idea of a passion play now seems quite sane. The notion of a Muslim month of mourning is even beginning to make sense. In the old days, regular bloodletting with leeches was considered the way to good health, a cleansing of the toxins. This is no longer in fashion, but in many ways these grief rituals seem to be its emotional counterpart. Iranians have survived a savage eight-year war, a revolution that dramatically changed the rules of social conduct, continuous limitation in their freedom of expression, and economic instability, and yet they remain resilient and good-spirited. Perhaps regular communal expression of sadness is their secret to survival.

Love,
Jasmine

April 17, 1998

My dear Jazz,

I figured I'd be caught once you made it to Iran. Thank the goddess, you're still speaking to me! I'm glad you appreciate my packages to your mother. Somehow, I knew you'd eventually come around to that. Jeez, I wish Belle were in good-enough shape to jump over flames. These days she's as round as Venus, and her knees are taking a toll. I offered to calculate her body mass index, but she was not amused. This does not bode well for my arthritic future. I tell you what I'd like to throw in those last Wednesday bonfires of yours. That's right, my diss! I'm so sick of it, I never want to look at it again. It's finally done, though. I never thought I'd live to see the day.

You're going to think I'm nuts, but I'm contemplating writing a novel starring, you guessed it, a little person. You'd think the last thing I'd want to do after finishing my diss is to embark on another writing project. But you know what? This book might actually make a difference in people's lives in contrast to my academic mumbo jumbo. I could market it on the LPA home page. You know, I'm finally ready to go to the LPA Convention this summer in L.A. I can shop the idea around. A few modern writers like Günter Grass, Armistead Maupin, and Ursula Hegi have done an impressive job of writing from the perspective of a dwarf, and there are even witty hunchback poems out there by Sandy Diamond approximating our experiences. But isn't it about time we represented ourselves in literary fiction?

I found the perfect title on the LPA Web site: "Against Tall Odds!" A damn shame it's already taken. I still miss Aria something terrible. I always will, Jasmine, but we all find our own ways of dealing. In the end, I think I want to share my experience with the world in the hopes that it may diminish the pain of another. It's amazing to see what's happened in my mentorship program.

Love you,
Dot

May 10, 1998

Dear Alexander,

You accompany me as I sit in my grandmother's old garden at dawn. Maman, Baba, and I have spent the night at what is now my uncle Hamid's house after a late-night birthday party for his granddaughter Rastak. The birthday girl will soon finish high school and then spend the next year studying for the college entry exam. Rastak is a serious student with hopes of becoming a doctor, but she has an infectiously joyous spirit that persuades even the nondancers of the family to get up with her and dance, including yours truly.

It was past 2 A.M. when we all went to bed, but I arose early, disappointed in my inability to connect with Aria in sleep. Of all days, I thought Mother's Day would be the cosmically correct time to have a reunion with her in my dreams. I wish her a joyful, would-have-been seventh birthday, wherever she may be and in whatever form.

In honor of her sweet tooth, I suck my black tea through a sugar cube, the traditional Iranian way, a surprisingly nice complement to the cardamom infusion. I would have never predicted that these ordinary inanimate objects would become the ambassadors to my dead daughter.

I spot a plain-looking bird. Its entire body from the little brown head with lighter ventral area to the reddish-brown tail could hide in a nest the size of my intertwining hands. It flies up and sits on the dark, glossy green foliage of a climbing white rosebush. Then it treats me to a solo performance: ethereal flute, ascending then spiraling down, hypnotizing the sleepy beetles and the fire ants. Its song is a love of total abandon and the cry of mothers, sad bells that continuously echo through my head.

Maman has also wakened early. She wraps a wool blanket around my shoulders, kisses my head, and goes back inside, presumably to pour herself a cup of tea.

I think of you often and have reread your beautiful letters on numerous occasions. Thank you, my dear Alexander, for not giving up on us. It would be unfair of me to promise you anything right now beyond accompanying you at Dot's hooding ceremony. Please save me a seat. Little Doctor Egyptology will be in for a big surprise.

Love,
Your Jasmine

Suddenly, the nightingale stops, flicking its wing and tail nervously, as if wary of being prey. I stop my breathing and speak only with my eyes: Sing, nightingale, sing.

This is a prayer, inchoate and unfinished,
for you, my love, my loss, my lesion,
a rosary of words to count out time's
illusions, all the minutes, hours, days
the calendar compounds as if the past
existed somewhere—like an inheritance
still waiting to be claimed.

—Dana Gioia

ACKNOWLEDGMENTS

I never planned to write a novel. A monsoon in Yogyakarta, Indonesia, trapped me indoors with little else to do other than contemplate the spiritually perplexing questions posed to me over the years by patients and family members. Thanks to a generous writing residency at Hedgebrook, a blissful reprieve in the midst of intense medical training, I found the perfect combination of solitude and community to transform my Indonesian musings into a coherent draft.

Laura Levine's creative writing course at Wellesley College was instrumental in making me believe I could write. Though I've never met them, Marilyn Sides and Carole Maso were influential in modeling the power and appeal of epistolary prose. Jack Laws, whom I came to know in a magical twist of fate thanks to this novel, corrected all of my nature references. Julie Gamble and the McPheeters family gave me valuable insight to Nebraska and graciously hosted me on their farm. Cynthia May Sheikholeslami provided helpful literature on the role of dwarfs in ancient Egypt. Katti Neshat and Maryam Neshat shared captivating stories about their Iranian ancestors. Azar Khajavi gave me erudite counsel on all matters related to language in Iran. Najmieh Batmanglij inspired me through her exquisite books on Persian cooking and culture. The Compassionate Friends parental bereavement support group and the Little People of America Web site were important research resources.

Special thanks to Joan Swift and Dana Gioia for use of their poems. The excerpted sonnet from "Letter from Hilo" from *The Tiger Iris* is copyright © 1999 by Joan Swift. Reprinted with permission of BOA Editions LTD. All rights reserved. The closing poem is an excerpt from "The Litany," copyright © 2001 by Dana Gioia. Reprinted from *Interrogations at Noon* with the permission of Graywolf Press, Saint Paul, Minnesota.

Revisions on the novel took more time than I care to recount, but could not have been possible without the quiet beauty of the Whiteley Center. I'm indebted to numerous friends who read the manuscript at various stages and invariably strengthened it with their commentary: Ahmad Karimi-Hakkak, Audrey Young, Claudia Mauro, Cynthia Liu, Daniel Rothenberg, Kate Noble, Leela Assefi, Mariam Shahriar, Mary Travers, Pinky Feria, Puwat Charukanoetkanok, Ricardo das Neves, Sandy Polishuk, Seema and Saul Clifasefi, Susie Frazier, and Tamar Halpern. Lisa Borders, with her astute editorial eye, went above and beyond the call of duty and thoroughly reviewed the manuscript on more than one occasion. Gitana Garofalo, who is not nearly as short as Dot, was the godsend midwife of this book, who coached it along during countless fits of preterm labor.

Several people provided moral support in the prepublication phase of *Aria* in the form of concrete suggestions and connections: Abolfazl Mehrabadi, Alexa Albert, Bingo Buchwald, Char Sundust, Chris de Bellaigue, Dedra Buchwald, Eve Rittenberg, Holly Morris, Jaideep Nair, Jeannette Farrell, Jenna Blum, Mariam Naini, Marshall Wolf, Reza Sheikholeslami, Rory Stewart, Sheryl Feldman, and Soheyla Gharib. *Aria* has benefited from the prodigious creativity of Niku Kashef and Bayesteh Ghaffary as well as from their gifts of loving friendship.

I feel like the luckiest writer alive to be represented by the amazing duo of Charlotte Sheedy and Violaine Huisman. Their warmth, generosity, intelligent guidance, and cutting-edge compassion have changed my life and have made the world a better place. It has been a pleasure and privilege to work with the quick brilliance, calming wisdom, and giant heart of my editor, Ann Patty. David Hough's meticulous copyediting is much appreciated, as is the behind-the-scenes work of the entire Harcourt team.

The resilience and good humor of my patients at Harborview Medical Center and in Afghanistan are a source of big-picture perspective, inspiration, and grace. I am blessed to have too many wonderful people in my life to list here, but heartfelt appreciation goes to all of my friends worldwide who've supported me during the long process of writing this book. *Mil besos para mi querido* Miguel Fernandez, *el ultimo de la fila* and master of the epistolary form; may we travel together *para siempre. Yek donya mamnoon* to my wonderful family in Iran and the diaspora. My parents, Homa and Touraj Assefi, deserve special praise for their patience with my unconventional life choices, and most notably for giving me an idyllic childhood, a hunger for travel, endless curiosity, and a love of children.